START ME UP

J. KENNER

Start Me Up

by

J. Kenner

Start Me Up Copyright © 2018 by Julie Kenner

Cover design by Covers by Rogenna

Cover image by Perrywinkle Photography

ISBN: 978-1-940673-74-5

Published by Martini & Olive Books

v. 2018_2_23P

Chapter One

"*GOOOOOD MORNING, AUSTIN,*" Nolan belted into the mike in his best Robin Williams impression. "It's six am on Wednesday, and if you thought you'd gotten up early enough to miss the traffic, then you're crazier than I am. It's a madhouse out there, but that's okay because it's crazy in here, too. But I'll be here to make your drive just a little more whacked, whether you're heading down the street or all the way across town."

He hit the switch on his console to pull up the *Twilight Zone* theme song, then leaned closer, deepened his voice, and channeled his inner Rod Serling. "It's the dimension between comedy and stupidity, between humor and idiocy. That's right, folks. I'm your host, Nolan Wood, and this is…" He paused for dramatic effect as his producer, Connor, increased the reverb on the sound effects, then finished on his show's title, "...*Mornings with Wood.*"

He'd been standing—it might only be six am, but Nolan was always revved before a show and he did his best work with a little bounce in his step—but now he fell back into his chair. He rolled a few feet to the back wall of the small, glassed-in studio as Connor cued the Satisfaction Sound Effect, a little clip Nolan had put together with rising applause that crescendoed on a woman's satisfied purr of, "Oh, Nolan!"

Then the drive-time show's theme music played, ending with the tag—recorded by one of the station's voice actors—"You're listening to *Mornings With Wood* on K-I-K-X Austin—kicks FM—at 96.3 on your radio dial. Classic music and classless chatter with your host, Nolan Wood."

In a rhythm as natural as sex, Nolan was back at the mike on cue, his body humming with energy as he slid into his schtick. "That's right, campers, it's a beautiful May morning. The sun is shining. The grass is green. The birds are singing. And there's one hell of a pile-up on southbound Mo-Pac near the Far West exit. Get off while you can, because that ain't pretty.

"And if you don't have an alternate route, well, I hope you like the sight of your dashboard, because other than the rear of the car in front of you, that's your view until you get off that highway to hell. And if that's not a good segue, I don't know what is. So here's a little AC/DC to wake you up and ease your pain."

As Nolan finished, Connor faded in *Highway to Hell*, and Nolan looked up with a grin. "Damn, but I love my job."

"Good," Connor shot back. "Because I sure as hell don't want it." He glanced down at the yellow pad that was never far from his side. "We're spinning into a commercial next, then where do you want to go? Requests? Naked News? Date-a-palooza?"

That's one of the reasons Nolan loved working with Connor. Nolan's last producer had insisted that he plan out the program in advance. But when Connor had stepped in nine months ago, Nolan had insisted the show would have more energy if Nolan had more leeway. He'd expected push-back, but the skinny former surfer from California had only shrugged and said that so long as he knew what was on the menu, he'd dig into whatever dish Nolan chose.

Honestly, if Connor had tits, Nolan would have dropped to one knee and proposed marriage right then. As it was, he took his new producer out for a drink at his favorite local bar, The Fix on Sixth, then exchanged life stories as they got rip-roaring drunk in that time-honored male-bonding ritual.

As for that marriage thing, it wouldn't have worked out, anyway. Gail—Connor's wife of five years—would never have approved. Then again, maybe she would. After all, unlike Nolan's ex, Gail had a killer sense of humor.

Frustrated, Nolan shook his head to clear out the unwelcome thoughts of Lauren. "Let's go with Come With Me," he suggested, referring to a new segment he'd only recently outlined.

Connor made a rough noise in his throat. "Ix-nay on that one until Mannie gives us the thumbs-up. He thinks you're going to push the line with too many orgasm jokes."

For the most part, the station's General Manager, Manuel Ortega, kept a loose rein on Nolan. But every once in a while he got a bug up his butt about a particular concept.

"It's a travel-themed call-in segment," Nolan protested. Which was, more or less, an entirely accurate statement. Heavy on the *less* side of that equation.

"So you're not going to choose the winner by deciding which of the callers convinces you they're coming right then? And I don't mean in the transportation sense of the word."

"How about we just go with Naked News, after all," Nolan suggested, aiming his most charming smile at his friend in order to avoid the question. "I feel the need to get visible."

Connor grinned, shaking his head in mock exasperation as he reached for his phone. When Nolan had first suggested live video streaming some segments on the station's social media platforms, Connor had been dubious. But the first time they'd tried it—with nothing more than Nolan behind the mike doing a riff—the ratings had zipped skyward and callers had tied up the phone lines for hours.

Never a sore loser, Connor had come to work the next day with a list of segments they could work into Nolan's usual routine. When he'd suggested Naked News, Nolan had clapped Connor on the shoulder, wiped away a fake tear, and told his friend he was as proud as a new father.

Now, Nolan rolled the segment's key prop—a picture of a bubble-filed bathtub painted on plywood —in front of his chair. Then he whipped off his shirt and sat down while Connor positioned the phone on a tripod at a ninety-degree angle to the prop.

Nolan was wearing sweatpants this morning. So for extra effect, he pulled the material up to bare his left leg, kicked off his shoe, and hooked his foot up onto the wooden edge of the fake tub. That put him too far away from his usual mike, but they'd installed pull-down mikes in four key places in the studio. He grabbed the one above him, tugged it down to the proper level, then grabbed the newspaper.

With just three seconds to go on the ad spot, Nolan leaned back into place. And as soon as the ad faded out, he slid in, telling his audience that it was time to get real with Naked News. "We wash away the dirt and leave you with nothing but the hard, clean truth behind the story. And we're doing it live," he added, to the applause and cheers of one of the show's many programmed sound effects.

He turned his head toward the camera as the streaming began, the result being that any listener not currently behind the wheel—and, sadly, probably a few that were—could hop over to the station's social media accounts and see what looked to be a naked Nolan sitting in a tub full of bubbles, with one leg hanging out, and a newspaper open in front of him. The paper, of course, remained miraculously dry.

One of the station's mandates was to keep listeners informed about local news, and even though the news department had that squarely in-hand, Connor reviewed the *Austin American-Statesman* every morning, then gave Nolan an oral report as part of Nolan's pre-show routine. Invariably, he found something in the news that he could turn into comedy gold.

Today was no exception, and he'd found fodder in an article about the city's recent hiring of a consulting firm to weigh in on the pros and cons of the city acquiring downtown historic property for preservation as museums and meeting spaces. "Don't these guys know that alcohol's a preservative? That makes Sixth Street one of the most preserved historic streets in the country. What the hell more do they want? And while we're at it, let's give away a couple of tickets to the upcoming Pink Chameleon concert in San Antonio. Just a little over a month away."

He held onto the arms of his chair, hidden from view, then pushed his body up so that his chest rose up out of the fake bubbles. At the same time, Connor hit the control for the low, breathy female voice. "Ooooh, Nolan! You're so big and strong! Tell me more!"

"Always happy to please," he said, grinning at the camera as he slid back into the chair and into the illusory bath bubbles. Usually, Connor made sure that Nolan had been briefed on at least five news items. Today, however, the second item on Connor's list had chilled Nolan, and he'd completely zoned out on the final three. Which was why Nolan was now confusing Connor by giving away the concert tickets far earlier in the program than his usual routine.

Well, too damn bad. Right then Nolan needed filler.

"Pink Chameleon's got a bright, shiny Grammy now, and the performance promises to be top-notch. Lead singer Kiki King's a local Austin gal, and I'm sure she'll be happy to be back in Texas for these two new additions to the tour schedule in Dallas and San Antonio. So how do you win? First caller with the original name of Austin's historic Sixth Street is our lucky concert-goer."

He started taking the calls—surprised by how many listeners were clueless. "Must've all moved here in the great California migration," he said to the camera. But then caller number six got it right—Pecan Street—and Nolan pulled an old-fashioned car horn out of his prop box, held it above tub level, and squeezed the bubble at the end to make the thing toot in victory.

"And that's it—" he began, in his vocal cue to Connor that the segment was over. But Connor, damn him, signaled for him to continue the Naked News skit, apparently because Connor was dealing with some sort of glitch on the control board.

Well, fuck. Because while Nolan was more than comfortable bullshitting his way through life and riffing off of any piece of news or gossip, the only other bit of news he'd heard in the briefing wasn't something he wanted to think about, much less talk about.

But there was no more news. Not unless Nolan wanted to skim the paper himself and parse out a story on-the-air. Since that wasn't happening, Nolan had to either dive into the news about his ex-wife Lauren and her shiny new husband ... or else he had to sit on dead air time.

And Nolan *never* had dead air on his show.

Screw it, he thought. And then he dove into the cold, deep waters of humiliation.

"This next bit of news is part public service announcement. Just a friendly reminder to all you unsuspecting folks out there to handle newspapers carefully. You never know when the words are going to reach out and bite you. Like this morning. See this?" He pointed to his neck. "Teeth marks. Big, gnarly, pointy teeth marks. The kind that are only left by wild animals and ex-wives."

Connor lifted his head, frowning. Nolan wasn't surprised. Nolan had been twenty-two when he and Lauren had split after six very non-blissful months. He was twenty-nine now, and he rarely thought of her. And he certainly didn't tend to mention her in passing. Even during drunken male-bonding marathons of debauchery.

"She and her Senator husband—and, yeah, I mean one of our United States senators from Texas— are apparently in town for a few different events, including a reception last night at the Governor's mansion. I sure hope there were ice sculptures at the reception. Would be a shame to waste those chilly ex-wife vibes."

He intended to stop there, but his mouth kept going. "But seriously, I wish them both my best. Of course, she always said my best wasn't very good. But you know what? I think she's wrong. I mean, look at me now."

He indicated the fake tub with a sweep of his hand, then pushed himself up again and used one hand to indicate a chest that he knew damn well women drooled for. "Naked *and* on the radio. I mean, come on. Can it really get much better than that? So you know what, babe? Here's all I have to say to you."

He turned his hand to flip the bird, and saw that Connor got the camera shut down just seconds before *that* image went out live. But, Nolan was sure, not fast enough to appease Mannie.

And then, in a move of pure programming genius, Connor manipulated the controls and killed Nolan's mike as he faded in the boisterous strains of Toby Keith's *How Do You Like Me Now*?!

"Fucking perfect," Nolan said.

"What the hell?" Connor retorted. "I brief you on that article, you don't even mention that the Senator's wife used to be yours?"

"Trust me, it wasn't worth mentioning."

Connor's eyes narrowed, as if he was trying to decide if Nolan meant it.

He did.

"She's gorgeous, and I was young and stupid. But we never meshed. She was a poor little rich girl, and all about her image. About making sure her whole life —and everyone in it—was picture perfect. When we were together, I thought she was a princess. And it took me a while to realize that she considered me a frog."

Before she'd walked out, she'd told him that she'd mistaken hot sex and multiple orgasms for love. That he was her walk on the wild side, and that it had been fun, but she wanted a man who would be somebody, and she should never have married him. Apparently, her idea of Prince Charming didn't include a high school drop-out who earned minimum wage as a file clerk and part-time board operator at a tiny AM station forty miles outside of Austin.

He shook his head, trying to knock the remnants of Lauren out of his brain. "It's better now. Mostly I hang with other frogs. And as for princesses…"

He trailed off with a shrug, thinking about all those gorgeous women who sought him out now because of his local celebrity. "I let them in my bed," he admitted, because Connor already knew that. And Nolan made damn sure that no woman he got horizontal with ever walked away unsatisfied or bemoaning his lack of sexual ambition. "But I'm not looking for anything serious."

He'd played the fool once. No way was he doing it again.

Chapter Two

"THIS IS SUCH A BAD IDEA," Shelby muttered as she slid out of Hannah's Mercedes and tried to stand upright on the unfamiliar four-inch heels.

"Nonsense," Hannah said, looking over the car's roof at Shelby. The copper highlights in her mass of blond curls gleamed in the late afternoon sun, shining as bright as Hannah's mischievous grin. "Bachelorette parties require the appropriate gift. And trust me, when it comes to honeymoon supplies, no place in Austin is better than Forbidden Fruit."

Shelby glanced at the pink storefront in the artsy North Loop shopping area. The name was spelled out in huge letters above a wall of windows that made Shelby wince, because anyone walking by would see her in there. And Shelby was really *not* the kind of girl to go into a sex toy store. Yes, she owned a vibrator, but she'd bought it the proper way—in secret from a mail order store that promised discreet packaging. And even then she'd waited two days to open the box, and had locked herself in her bedroom before using her manicure scissors to slice through the packing tape.

All that, despite the fact that she lived alone and no one else had been in her house. But about some things, you really couldn't be too careful.

Hannah only laughed and shook her head as she came around the car to take Shel by the elbow. "You can do it. Come on. Consider it a life milestone. One wacky thing to check off your bucket list."

"Wacky is right," Shelby muttered, as she tottered alongside her friend wishing she was still wearing her comfortable pumps and her familiar linen blend suit with the skirt that hit just below the knee. But no. She was about to walk into a sex shop wearing Fuck Me pumps and a skin-tight little black dress she'd borrowed from Hannah with a slit that extended from the knee-length hem all the way up to mid-thigh. They were the same height, but whereas Hannah was trim and athletic, Shelby had definite curves, which the lycra-cotton blend was clinging to like plastic wrap.

She was also wearing thong panties in defense against panty lines, and her legs were bare. Which, considering that Shelby was used to pantyhose, was a rather disconcerting experience, as she was feeling a definite breeze in places where there usually wasn't one.

Seriously, why had she listened to Hannah? Because now Shelby was about to walk into a sex toy shop dressed like she was there to buy professional supplies.

"You owe me big time," she said to Hannah.

"Fair enough. Now come on. It's already almost seven and we have to get back downtown to meet the girls at eight."

The bachelorette party was for Celia James, one of the secretaries at Brandywine Finance & Consulting, the firm where Shelby worked as a financial advisor and where Hannah served as in-house counsel. It was a low-key, mid-week affair, as Celia's college friends had taken her to Cancun for her official party. When Shelby had pointed that out to Hannah in support of the argument that work clothes—or even jeans and a blazer—would be perfectly fine, Hannah had pulled out her best friend veto power.

"Fine," Shelby said now. "But I'm still not staying late. I have to work tomorrow."

"We all have to work tomorrow," Hannah retorted, then held the glass door open. "Come on."

With a sigh, Shelby did as she was told, her eyes widening as she stood in the center of the cavernous room scoping out the displays. Walls of vibrators and dildoes. Cases of lube. Sections with handcuffs and blindfolds and other restraints. And leather. Lots of leather.

A woman with a friendly smile greeted them, asking if they needed help, but Hannah assured her they were fine. Shelby said nothing, although she may have made a small squeaking noise. It wasn't that she was a prude. She'd had sex—and not only in the missionary position, either.

But all of this was so very *public*.

At first, she stuck close to Hannah. But when her friend called the clerk over to explain the pros and cons of various vibrators, Shelby drifted away, finding herself near a glass case with leather handcuffs, a fur blindfold, and a roll of something that looked like electrical tape.

She bit her lower lip as her gaze skimmed over the display. A pleasant tingle started below her belly button, and she tried to imagine being naked in bed, the mask over her eyes, and her arms taped to the headboard.

She could almost feel the pressure of a man's hands on her, rough and strong as he roamed down her skin to cup her at the waist, and then the heat of his mouth on her breasts as he—

"Can I answer any questions?"

Shelby actually yelped, then teetered on her heels as she tried to steady herself. "I—um—no. I'm just waiting for my friend."

"Feel free to look around," the saleswoman said. "And if you need any help, just let me know."

"Oh. Sure. Absolutely."

The woman started to turn away, and Shelby surprised herself by saying, "Actually, what is this?" She was pointing to the roll of electrical tape. "Wouldn't that, like, hurt?"

The woman shook her head, her expression kind and professional. "It only sticks to itself. So it won't pull on your skin or leave a residue," she said. "Much more portable than handcuffs, and infinitely more versatile."

"Ohhhh!" Hannah said, coming up behind them. "Toss a roll in for me, would you?" She winked at Shelby. "We're going to make sure Celia has the best honeymoon ever. And then I think that'll do it," she told the saleswoman.

"Wonderful. Just meet me at the register when you're ready."

Hannah nodded, then nudged Shelby. "Looking for a little something for yourself? I mean, there's always Alan, right…"

Shelby frowned, thinking about Alan Lowe, the assistant professor she'd been dating ever since her mother had introduced them three months ago, assuring her that the two of them would be perfect together. And they were. Alan was sweet and polite and thoughtful. And the two times they'd slept together had been perfectly fine. But—

She shook her head. "I don't think bondage tape is Alan's thing."

Hannah's lips thinned as she very obviously held back a laugh.

"What?"

"I just find your word choice interesting. Not *Alan's* thing? Does that mean it is yours?"

Shelby rolled her eyes. "Oh, please," she said. "Go pay, and let's get out of here."

Hannah glanced at her watch. "Shit. We really do need to get going." As she hurried toward the checkout, Shelby glanced one more time at the cuffs and tape.

Definitely not Alan's thing, but even though they'd never actually talked about being exclusive, Alan was the only guy on Shelby's current radar.

So who was the man in her delicious little fantasy? For that matter, why was she fantasizing at all? She was perfectly happy with Alan and their casual non-relationship. Maybe they were moving more slowly than was common these days, but there was nothing wrong with that.

"Getting back to Alan," Hannah began, once they were in her car and heading toward downtown. "Obviously he's not tying you up and fucking you like crazy—"

"Hannah!"

"—so what *is* going on with you two?"

"Oh, my God," Shelby said, a little disconcerted

that Hannah's question tracked Shelby's own. Albeit in a completely mortifying way. "You're impossible."

"I know. I really am. It's just so easy to tease you. But the question's legit. You and I haven't had the chance to catch up in weeks. I do want to know what's going on with you."

Shelby lifted a shoulder, a little mollified. "Alan's great. He's the perfect guy. Smart. Attractive. And he's on tenure track at the university." Alan was an assistant professor at UT in the same department where her mother held a tenured position as a professor in the Department of Statistics and Data Sciences. And her father, who was a high-level statistician with the State of Texas, thought that Alan pretty much hung the moon.

"Mom says he'll probably be the dean of the department someday," Shelby added.

"And?"

"And what?"

"Oh, come on, Shel. Forget bondage tape—but does he get your motor revving?"

Shelby smirked. "My motor is doing just fine. And a good relationship is about more than sex, anyway." Alan was kind, smart, well-read, and they enjoyed so many of the same things, like concerts and classic movies and quiet nights at home.

All in all, Shelby and Alan made sense. The same way that a balanced equation made sense. And just like in math, Shelby could see the way the formula played out. Two more months of casually seeing each other, and then they'd talk about being exclusive. Six months after that, they'd get engaged. They'd get married in the summer, and by next winter, she'd be Mrs. Alan Lowe.

Hannah shot a quick glance at Shelby before checking her mirror and changing lanes. "I just —never mind."

"What?"

"Nothing. I swear. It's just that—well, I don't want to see you settle."

"Dating Alan is *not* settling. He's the kind of guy who'll make the perfect husband and father."

"You're getting married?"

"Well, not now, obviously. But I think Alan definitely checks all the boxes."

Hannah's brows lifted. "Does he check *your* box?"

"What's that supposed to mean?"

"I only want you to have fun."

Shelby sat up straighter. "I have fun. Just because I don't sleep around doesn't mean I don't have fun."

"Oh, hell," Hannah said. "You know I didn't mean it like that."

Shelby slumped back in the seat. "I know," she said. And she did. Her whole life she'd been juggling well-meaning friends who saw her as shy or sedate or boring or too much of a brainiac to have any social skills. And maybe that was true. But that didn't mean she wasn't happy, because she was. Happy and ambitious and successful.

More than that, Shel knew exactly what she wanted in both her career and her life.

With her career, Shel had been obsessed with numbers since the first time her dad sat her down and taught her the multiplication tables. The way they worked, what they represented, the streamlined beauty of the truth they represented.

Accounting suited her perfectly. Not only was she helping people and companies, but she got to play in that finite world that always made sense. Because at the end of the day—at least in the world of accounting—two plus two always equaled four.

As for her life, she wanted a home like the one she'd grown up in, with respect and security and a partner who was both ambitious and loyal to his family. Someone who took life and relationships seriously.

Shelby knew only too well what could go wrong if you didn't walk that line. Her mother's brother—her uncle—had never had any real ambition, and he'd ended up divorced and in rehab after his band had broken up.

And her cousin Violet on her father's side had gone off and married a stand-up comedian who convinced her he was going to be the next big sitcom star. Now they fought all the time and lived in a tiny apartment in Los Angeles with three kids. And her husband managed a local fast-food restaurant.

Not Shelby. She wasn't going to be stupid about her life—and she wasn't succumbing to what felt like a family curse. Her parents had managed to find the right path, and she intended to walk right in their footsteps.

Maybe it didn't sound sexy, but to Shelby, the kind of financial security, ordered life, and familial affection that her parents shared was what defined a life well-lived. The kind of life she wanted for herself.

The kind of life that a man like Alan would fit into perfectly.

So why was she was fantasizing about bondage tape? Especially when the anonymous man in her fantasy was absolutely, totally, one hundred percent *not* Alan Lowe?

Chapter Three

"OH, my God! You guys are terrible!" Celia pulled the purple vibrator and black bondage tape out of the pink gift bag with *Bride-To-Be* emblazoned on the side, then held them up for everyone to see. And not only the bachelorette party guests. No, to Shelby's utter mortification, pretty much every customer, server, and bartender in The Fix on Sixth also turned to look.

"Brian is going to absolutely love our wedding night. Thank you both," Celia added, aiming her crooked, drunken grin at both Hannah and Shelby.

"Um, Celia?" Shel tugged on her co-worker's sleeve. "The whole bar is staring."

But Celia just laughed, yanked her arm free, and brandished the purple contraption even more wildly over her head.

"Come on, Shel," Celia said, her words slurring together. "I'm getting married. Nobody cares about this." She poked Shel in the chest with the vibrator's silicon tip. "They're all just happy for me. Even them," she added, using the sex toy as a pointer while her arm swept the room to encompass all the tables in the main area of The Fix.

A few of the customers laughed outright, but most had the grace to turn away from the drunk and crazy bride-to-be. And Shelby—already too far down the rabbit hole to climb out—decided that it was time to either leave the party or surrender all pretense of decorum.

She weighed both options for only a second, then made her selection. "Pass me the pitcher, will you?" she asked Hannah, to general whoops of approval. "I *so* need another drink."

The group of six women had set up the bache-lorette party at the large table by the window at the front of The Fix, right beside the colorful wall mural depicting Austin. They had a fabulous view of the pedestrians on Sixth Street, many of whom slowed to gape at the pretty bride in her gaudy, bejeweled BRIDE tiara. Not to mention the assorted selection of anatomically correct candies and cakes that dotted the table, courtesy of Naughty Cakes, a local bakery.

By the time Celia finished opening all the presents and the girls had devoured a platter of penis cupcakes, they'd also polished off three entire pitchers of Pinot Punch—a wine, Schnapps, and frozen peach concoction that the cute bartender had promised they'd love. He hadn't lied, and as the liquid in the pitchers decreased, the noise level rose in an almost mathematically predictable ratio.

Now, the din in little corner of The Fix had increased to DEFCON Rowdy.

"I'm totally serious," Shelby assured her rapt audience of tipsy women. She adjusted her glasses, then took another sip from her fourth—no, fifth—glass of punch, then continued the story she'd been telling about a local country and western singer who'd hit her up for advice not long after she'd passed her CPA exam. "He told me they were a business expense. Said they relaxed him so that he could hear the music in his head."

"Butt plugs?" Celia asked, her eyes wide. "Vibrating butt plugs were his muse?"

"You want to say that a little louder?" Leslie from payroll said. "I don't think that table on the far side of the room heard you."

"What did you do?" Celia asked.

"Nothing. I told you, he was just chatting me up at a party. But I can't listen to his music anymore. At least not without wondering how he wrote it."

Hannah laughed so loud she practically snorted. "I can't believe you haven't told me this story before."

Shelby shrugged. Honestly, she couldn't believe she was telling it now. But her mind and her tongue seemed pleasantly loose. She knew it was the punch— most of the time she never drank anything stronger than Perrier with lime when she went out. Not only did she hate having to rely on someone else to get her home—whether a friend or a taxi or a ride share app—she just plain didn't like feeling out of control.

But today was a special occasion, and it felt nice to be laughing and drinking and having a good time with her friends.

"I'm so happy for you," she said, leaning over to hug Celia.

"Thanks! And I know—"

Celia cut herself off, her eyes going wide as she gripped Shelby's wrist. "Don't look toward the bar," she whispered. "But that guy is watching you again."

"Really?" She was facing the window, and now she twisted in her seat to get a view of the long oak bar that ran parallel to the interior wall of the bar's main room.

Celia jerked her back. "I said don't look!"

"Oh, right," Shelby said, but she felt her cheeks go pink, because she'd gotten enough of a glimpse to know that the cute guy with the short dark hair and pale gray eyes really was looking her direction. "He's not looking at me," Shel protested.

"Please, girlfriend," Hannah said, scooting closer, "he totally is. And why wouldn't he? You look hot. The outfit is amazing. And so is your hair and make-up, if I do say so myself."

Hannah lived in one of the many downtown condos that had popped up in Austin over the last decade. Instead of going straight for The Fix after Forbidden Fruit, she'd insisted on a quick pit stop, during which Hannah had changed out of her short skirt and into skintight jeans and a backless silk halter. After that, she'd touched up Shelby's make-up and then worked a little magic on her hair. "We may be ten minutes late," she'd said. "But we'll make one hell of an entrance."

Before, Shel had pinned her hair up so that a few tendrils framed her face. She'd been pleased with the effect and had thought that Hannah had approved.

"It's great," Hannah had assured her as she'd yanked out the pins and fired up her curling iron. "But this will be better."

And it was. She'd pulled down Shelby's shoulder-length dark hair, then proceeded to curl each and every strand with a large diameter curling iron. The result being a mass of curls that framed her face and bounced when she walked.

"Even your glasses look great," Hannah had added, tilting her head as she examined Shelby critically. "The aqua color's really fun, and it brings out the blue in your eyes." Shelby's eyes were hazel, and tended to pick up the color of whatever she was wearing.

Now, in The Fix, Hannah looked her over once again with approval. "I think it's the glasses coupled with that killer outfit that caught his eye. You're welcome, by the way. It gives you a studious minx look."

"You realize you sound like you're casting a porn video, right?" Shelby protested, making all the girls at the table laugh.

"Whatever," Celia said. "But Hannah's right. The point is that Mr. Hottie likes it. I mean, did you see the way he was watching you earlier? Like he could totally eat you up."

Shelby's face flushed warm. "That's because you tossed me that stupid vibrator. He looked over at us right as I caught the thing." She'd been holding the purple device in both hands, and she'd glanced up to see Mr. Hottie's eyes locked on her. Pale gray and deep set, with the kind of long lashes some women paid a lot of money for. *Bedroom eyes*, Shelby thought, then quickly banished the ridiculous thought.

She remembered the way the corner of his mouth had quirked up as he'd watched her—not to mention the corresponding tug she'd felt deep inside. She'd looked away, then, suddenly shaky and dry-mouthed and unsure.

"He was laughing at me," she said, "not lusting for me." But the protest sounded false even to her own ears. There'd been a definite *zing* between them. But that didn't mean Shel was going to do anything about it. And even if she was inclined to pull on that thread, she honestly didn't know what to do or how to do it.

"Well, he's not laughing now," Celia said. "That's some serious lust in those eyes."

"You should go talk to him," Hannah said.

A shock of terror cut straight through Shelby. "Are you insane?"

"Hannah's right," Celia said. "You should."

Shelby tried to shake her head, but it came off as more of a trembling chin wiggle. "No way. *Really*. No. Freaking. Way."

"Oh, come on, Shelby. He's obviously interested." Hannah nudged her shoulder. "I'll go with you if you want. He's by the bar. We could go order a drink. Strike up a conversation."

"A drink? Another drink and I'll float away. In fact, I need the ladies' room." The combination of alcohol and nerves actually made the need rather urgent, and her stomach began to roil. "Oh, God," she said, clapping her hand over her mouth as she stood and stumbled toward the back of the bar.

"Oh, hell," she heard Hannah say, followed by the scrape of a chair. Then her friend was at her side, and they were hurrying to the restroom, and Shelby was fighting the ridiculous urge to laugh, because this *never* happened to her. And as mortifying as the whole thing was, she was really and truly having one heck of a good time.

They reached the restroom, and Shelby pushed the door. It was lighter than she expected, and it slammed in, banging against the back wall and making Shelby jump and someone inside the bathroom yelp. She caught Hannah's eye, and they both started laughing like loons.

"Come on," Hannah said, hooking an arm around Shelby's waist and leading her inside. Shelby stumbled, then looked up at Hannah as her head swam. "The floor is moving," she announced, suddenly realizing how much she'd had to drink. She hadn't felt it when she'd been sitting down. But now that she was up and moving … *whoa, Nellie.*

She drew in a breath, but the extra oxygen didn't help much. She lifted her head, stared down all four of Hannah's eyes, and said as slowly and clearly as she could manage, "I totally blame you."

From across the small room, she heard a little gasp, followed by, "Shelby?"

Shelby blinked, then tried to focus on the pretty blonde standing by the sink. It took a second, and then it hit her, and Shelby grinned so wide it almost hurt. "Brooke Hamlin!" She stumbled toward the other woman, then threw her arms out and engulfed her in a hug.

Shelby had worked on the Hamlin family's taxes since before she took the CPA exam. Technically, her former boss was Judge Hamlin's accountant, but Shel had done the heavy lifting and had met everyone in the family on more than one occasion.

In fact, she and Brooke were close to the same age

and had met for lunch once or twice after tax season was over.

Now, Shelby added an extra squeeze to her boisterous hug. "Isn't this the best party?" she said, not remembering that Brooke wasn't actually at their party until she responded with a dubious, "Um, yeah?"

Beside them, Hannah laughed as she thrust out her hand for Brooke to shake. "Hannah," she said in introduction. "Also known as Shelby's babysitter."

"Like hell," Shelby retorted, fully intending to explain why she didn't need a babysitter. Unfortunately, some Pinot Punch came up with her words, and so she clapped her hand over her mouth and stumbled toward the open stall, then locked the door behind her before crouching down as her stomach betrayed her.

She stayed on her haunches, breathing through her mouth just in case her stomach decided to go another round. Outside the stall, she heard Brooke and Hannah talking, and she rolled her eyes at Brooke's comment that there must have been an alien invasion because, "That's not Shelby."

"Isn't it awesome?" Hannah asked, her voice positively giddy. "We're here for a friend's bachelorette party, and I told Shel she had to let her hair down."

"You're evil," Shel called from the stall, then chuckled at Hannah's immediate retort of, "But you love me!"

While Hannah and Brooke continued to talk, Shel gathered herself, finally emerging when she was sure that she and the punch left in her stomach had come to an understanding. "Whoa," she said, heading for the sink and the dispenser of complimentary mouthwash. "I feel better."

And she did, too. The room was spinning less, and her head felt much more clear. Once she swished and spit, she felt positively human.

Hannah's lips twitched, and Shelby pointed an accusatory finger at her, but Hannah just hid her laugh behind a fake cough before turning to Brooke and asking if she'd like to join them.

"No, thanks. I need to get going."

"You sure?" Shelby pulled her into a one-armed hug. "Because it's really so awesome to see you."

"You, too," Brooke said, and from the way she laughed, Shel was sure that Brooke thought she was still drunk. Which maybe she was. A little, anyway.

"Come on," Brooke added. "I'll walk out with you, at least."

They traipsed out together, moving through the crowd toward the front corner where the laughing, drinking group of bachelorette party-goers now waved at Shelby and Hannah, urging them to hurry back because the bartender, Cam, had delivered two more pitchers of that deliciously dangerous punch.

Of course, the shortest way back was to walk parallel to the bar, and that put her right in front of the group of men with whom Mr. Hottie had been hanging.

Shelby told herself she shouldn't look, but she couldn't help it, and the next thing she knew, she was bumping into Brooke as she reached for Hannah's arm and pulled her to a stop. "He's still there," she whispered, shooting a surreptitious glance toward Mr. Hottie. "Do you think he's—*oh, shit*. He's looking this way."

Those eyes. He'd just completely nailed her with those gorgeous eyes. And, yes, Shelby was still a little loaded, but she felt the impact of that look all the way down to her toes. And she was pretty sure it wasn't because of the alcohol.

"Just go talk to him." Hannah gave her a little shove, but Shelby wasn't about to budge. "He's obviously noticed you. And you have *so* noticed him."

"Who?" Brooke asked, and Shelby whipped around to face her, mortified that someone other than Hannah had witnessed her moment of lust.

"Him," Hannah said, but before she could lift a finger to point, Shelby yanked her arm down, almost losing her balance in the process. Four-inch heels and Pinot Punch were not a safe combination.

"Don't point! The cute guy right there," she told Brooke. "With the short hair and the *The best mornings have Wood* T-shirt."

Then Brooke did the unthinkable. She raised her hand and actually waved at the guy.

"Oh. My. God." Shelby wanted to melt into the floor right then. Was Brooke insane? "Why are you waving at him?"

Brooke shrugged, totally nonplussed. "He's a friend. His name's Nolan Wood. And the tacky shirt is the name of his show. *Mornings With Wood*. He does crazy ass commentary for one of the local radio stations."

"You know him?"

"Casually. He was going out with a friend."

"Oh." A disconcerting wave of disappointment crashed over Shelby. Ridiculous, since it wasn't as if she intended to go out with the guy. He just happened to be very pleasant to look at.

"He's single now, I think," Brooke continued, her tiny smile suggesting that she understood Shel's disappointment. Except, of course, that Shel hadn't been disappointed.

Really.

"Just go," Hannah urged before turning to Brooke. "I keep telling her to go introduce herself and say hi."

Brooke looked from Hannah to Shelby. "I can introduce you."

She said more after that, but those four little words had taken up all the space in Shelby's brain, and she didn't hear anything else until Hannah gave her a little shove in the direction of the men.

"Yes. Perfect. Go."

"But—"

"Go," Hannah repeated as the band playing on the stage at the other side of the room ended their set and people started to shuffle toward the bar.

"We'll all go," Brooke said, beginning to thread her way through the increasing crowd. Shelby followed for a bit, but then her nerves got the better of her and she held back, despite Hannah's persistent urging.

After a moment, Brooke paused, turned around, and then headed back toward Shelby and Hannah with an amused smile playing at her lips.

"I can't believe you were going to walk right over to him," Shelby said.

"Well, I thought I was going with you," Brooke replied. She said something else, too, but a rowdy frat boy shouting at his friend blocked all but Brooke's last words. "He doesn't bite."

"At least not unless you ask him to," Hannah quipped.

"I really can't," Shelby said. "I mean isn't it..." She shook her head and drew a deep breath. "I'm not usually so bold. Are you?" she demanded, wishing she could get into Brooke's head. The other woman seemed so confident.

"Me?"

Shelby nodded. "Yeah. Would you ever throw caution to the wind like that?"

Brooke's expression turned wistful. And maybe a little sad. "I have," she said. "I did."

"Oh." Shelby and Hannah exchanged glances. "What happened?"

Brooke blinked. "I fell in love," she said, her voice thick with emotion.

"Careful," Hannah teased. "You might scare her off."

Brooke shook her head, as if clearing her thoughts, then smiled at Shel. "Go talk to him." She started to raise her hand to signal Mr. Hottie, but then she froze. For a moment, she simply stood there, and Shelby finally realized that she was staring at a good-looking bearded man holding a highball glass.

She turned back to Shelby and Hannah, her expression a little shell-shocked. "I—I forgot some-thing in the ladies' room. Y'all go on ahead. Nolan's a really nice guy. Just introduce yourself."

"What—" Shelby began, but Brooke hurried away before she could finish the question, and Shelby was left standing beside Hannah, more than a little baffled.

"What was that about?" Hannah asked, but Shelby could only shrug.

"Come on. Celia's probably wondering what we're doing."

"Oh, no," Hannah said, grabbing Shelby's wrist. "Just because you lost your wingman does not mean you have to abandon your mission."

Shelby blinked, her mind too fuzzy to make sense of Hannah's words.

"I mean *go*," Hannah said. "You're a gorgeous, smart, interesting woman fueled by liquid courage. There is no reason why you can't walk up to the guy, smile at him, and ask if he wants to buy you a drink."

"But—"

Hannah put her hand on her hip and stared Shelby down. "But what?"

Shelby had intended to point out that she really didn't need another drink. Instead, she shook her head. "Nothing."

She swallowed, then glanced toward the guy. *Nolan.* Brooke said his name was Nolan. He'd shifted to make room for the newcomers at the bar, so he was no longer looking her direction. But as if he felt her eyes on him, he tilted his head a bit to the side. And then, very slowly, he looked over his shoulder.

Zing!

His eyes found hers immediately, and in that instant, she forgot how to breathe. Her chest tightened, and her skin prickled from the electricity arcing between them. And for one breathless, wonderful moment, she lost herself in the fantasy of his touch. His hands on her waist. His breath on her neck. His lips at her mouth.

Good grief, she really was drunk.

The thought slammed against her, and she took an involuntary step backward. And it was only when she stumbled on those damn four-inch heels that she realized he'd moved from his place at the bar to right in front of her. He reached out, one hand taking her elbow and the other sliding around her waist to keep her from falling. As if she hadn't fallen hard already.

"I've got you," he said, his rich, low voice as intimate as a caress.

Some tiny sober corner of her mind pointed out that Hannah had slipped back to the party. That Shelby was alone with Nolan. That Nolan was holding her close, probably feeling her heartbeat.

That this was her chance—and she'd damn sure never get another one.

She drew in a trembling breath as she gathered her courage, searching for the perfect words for this perfect moment.

"I'm sorry," she blurted, as intellect and moxie both failed her completely. "But you really need to let me go."

Chapter Four

NOLAN LEANED AGAINST THE BAR, a longneck in one hand and his eyes on his dark-haired paradox.

A regular at The Fix, he'd come tonight to wash away the bad taste that had been lingering on his tongue ever since Connor had briefed him on the news that Lauren was in town. The beer hadn't made a dent, but the girl … *wowza*.

It wasn't every day that a woman captured Nolan's attention so completely.

And it *really* wasn't every day that a woman ran from him. On the contrary, ever since the station had put his face on a few billboards and Connor had set up the live streaming on his social media accounts, not a day went by that he wasn't propositioned.

Nice for his ego—except when it wasn't. Because Nolan knew damn well that those women only wanted a piece of his celebrity, however minor and local it might be.

That, and his cock.

Not this girl, though…

She, apparently, didn't want him at all. Despite spending much of the evening stealing glances at him and blushing a pretty shade of pink.

The girl was a paradox, that was for sure. And one he desperately wanted to solve.

"Earth to Nolan. You still with us, man?"

Nolan glanced over at Reece Walker, who'd sidled up beside him, a beer of his own in his hand. "You know that girl?" He nodded toward the dark-haired paradox. Considering Reece managed the bar, if anyone recognized her, it would probably be Reece.

Reece ran his hand over his shaved scalp as he studied the scene. "Sorry. Haven't seen her in here before." He tilted his head back, indicating the bartender. "You ask Cameron?"

Nolan nodded. "No luck there, either. He's seen a few of the girls once or twice, but not the one in the aqua glasses." He took a sip of beer, then swallowed. "That's okay," he added, shooting his friend a wry glance. "I have my ways."

Reece chuckled, but didn't comment. Nolan figured that was for the best. He'd known Reece most of his adult life, ever since Nolan's stepsister Amanda had shared a dorm room with Jenna Montgomery, one of Reece's best friends. And after so many years, Reece knew Nolan just a little too well.

"By the way," Reece asked, "did Jenna talk to you about doing some shout-outs for The Fix on your show?"

Nolan nodded. "Just in passing. We planned for her to come to the studio sometime this week to talk details and review some sound effects for the spots. But Amanda filled me in when I saw her at Mom and Huey's on Sunday."

Jenna had been in a rush when she'd explained that the bar was in a financial crisis and that they could really use his help getting the word out about some new promotions and events they had going on to try to increase revenue. He'd told her to count him in for whatever they needed, and they'd planned to talk more seriously at the KIKX studio.

Then, when Amanda had told him the details about what Jen wanted him to promote, he'd laughed so hard, he'd almost spit out the Scotch and soda his stepfather had made him as a pre-dinner cocktail.

"And you're sure it's cool?" Reece pressed. "With the station? With you? We could really use the publicity for the bar and the contest."

"Are you kidding? It's like an avalanche of comedy gold. Guys strutting shirtless across a stage to be in a calendar. Hell, yes, I'm in."

"Good. Just remember the idea is to draw the customers in, not scare them off."

Nolan held up a hand in the Boy Scout salute. "I promise to treat the whole thing with the respect it deserves."

Reece rolled his eyes. "Maybe you should enter the contest. That really would be funny."

"Nice. Very nice."

Reece just clapped him on the back, thanked him for helping out, then told Cam to comp his drinks. Sometimes, it really was good to have friends.

At the moment, though, he was wishing that his dark-haired paradox didn't have quite so many. She was still surrounded by bachelorette party-goers who showed no signs of slowing down, despite the fact that it was almost midnight on a work night.

He frowned, cursing the gaggle of girls. He wanted to get her alone. He wanted to taste those lips. Hell, he wanted to ask her why she'd bolted.

He set his empty bottle aside, then signaled to Cam for another. As he waited, he leaned back, his arms crossed over his chest as he considered the problem. Hell, maybe he should just walk away. Maybe she wasn't interested in him at all.

But then she turned, her eyes finding him before darting away again, as if he was her guilty little secret. He bit back a self-satisfied grin. Because he'd figured something out. She wasn't *playing* hard to get. She *was* hard to get.

And that was all Nolan needed to know.

Fighting a grin, he turned around to take the fresh

bottle from Cameron, then he put in a brand new order, too. A little bit of ammunition for his spur of the moment plan.

A few minutes later, he watched as one of the waitresses approached the dark-haired woman with a tall glass full of ice, a clear liquid, and a twist of lime. His paradox frowned, clearly confused, then listened as the waitress pointed in Nolan's general direction. Then his paradox's brow furrowed and she pointed to her friends and their cluster of tables, now littered with a slew of drained glasses and half-empty Pinot Punch pitchers.

He couldn't hear what they were saying, but he knew she was protesting that she'd had enough to drink already. And when he saw the perfect lips on that gorgeous wide mouth form the words, "I can't," it was almost as if he could hear her sweet, sexy purr.

Her blonde friend came to her side just as the waitress was explaining something. He saw his paradox frown, clearly confused, and then he saw her friend's smile widen in what could only be pure, devious delight.

Then his paradox turned his direction, and when their eyes met, he was struck with a wave of such pure desire that he almost put a stop to his whole ridiculous plan right then. It had been one hell of a long time since he'd craved a woman this much, and he wasn't much sure he liked the feeling.

Then again, maybe he liked it too much.

By the party tables, the blonde gave his paradox a little shove, and she stumbled forward, unsteady on those heels, which were clearly her nemesis despite doing amazing things for her legs and ass.

She turned her head, but this time it wasn't to look at him. Instead, she was glancing the opposite direction, back toward her friends, all of whom were nodding encouragement and shooting him surreptitious glances while he pretended to be too occupied with peeling the label off his beer to notice.

Still, as she headed his direction, he decided that he liked each and every one of her friends, and if the whole group wasn't already wasted, he would have bought them a fresh round of drinks. As it was, he slipped Cam a card for a taxi service he often used, and told the bartender to keep him anonymous, but to make sure each of the girls knew that their ride home was taken care of.

He turned back just in time to find his paradox walking the last few feet toward him. He wanted to watch her approach—the little swivel in her hips, way her teeth grazed her lower lips, the way she fisted her hands, then wiped her palms on that deliciously sexy skintight black dress—but she was so obviously nervous and confused that he had to go to her. Had to reassure her. And so he pushed away from the bar and met her halfway, feeling unfamiliarly nervous himself.

"You bought me club soda," she said, and from

her tone it was impossible to tell if she was asking a question or making an accusation.

"I wanted to buy you a drink," he admitted. "But I thought wine or more Schnapps-laced punch might be counterproductive."

"Oh." She licked her lips, and he had to tighten his grip on the beer so that he didn't bend forward and taste that mouth right then. "Um, to what?"

"To the fact that I want to kiss you." He wanted to do a hell of a lot more than that, but he didn't want to scare her away. "And when I do, I want you sober."

"Oh," she said again. "Well, that's too bad."

"Why's that?" He held his breath, afraid she was going to tell him that she wasn't interested in either him or a pick-up line.

But then he saw her throat move as she swallowed. And when she lifted her head, and he saw the courage gathered in those blue-gray eyes, his cock tightened in response to a flood of desire so potent it almost brought him to his knees.

"Because I'm incredibly drunk," she finally said. "And I really don't want to wait to be kissed."

Chapter Five

SHELBY'S EYES went wide and she took a step back as her hand flew up to her mouth. *Had she really just said that? Surely she hadn't really said that.*

Except she had. She could tell by the heat that had flared in his eyes in response to her words—an ember that had flashed into flame as quickly and dramatically as if she'd thrown a match into a pool of gasoline.

Never again. She was never, ever, *ever* drinking again.

"I don't…" she began, then trailed off uncertainly. Maybe she didn't, but she damn sure wanted to.

"Don't you?" There were small lines at the corners of his eyes and she knew he was laughing at her. And, strangely, instead of irritating her, his reaction relaxed her. "And too bad if you don't," he continued. "Because I bet you do it very well."

"Kissing?" she asked, so hyperaware of him that every tiny hair on her body seemed to dance with electricity. And her lips—oh, dear God, her lips tingled with unanswered promises, delicious and shiny and forbidden.

He leaned close, his breath tickling her ear as he whispered, "Everything."

"Oh." She swallowed, wondering how one simple word had the power to melt her. And not even a word that made sense. Because somehow they'd entirely lost the thread of the conversation.

Or had they?

She didn't know. Her mind was all muddled, and she was *never* muddled. Shelby prided herself on being a very unmuddled person.

It had to be the alcohol. She should be embarrassed, not intrigued. Nervous, not turned on. But there was something about him. Something about the way he looked at her. The way she felt simply standing beside him.

With supreme effort, she tried again to wrap her head around the conversation. "I meant that I don't usually *flirt*."

"Really? I'm surprised. Especially since you're doing such a great job." His gray eyes danced as she cocked her head, staring him down.

He laughed, holding his hands up in a defensive

gesture. "Maybe it's the Pinot Punch. That stuff packs quite a kick."

She nodded seriously, grateful he understood. "Yes."

He took a step closer, and she breathed in his cologne. Something woodsy with just a hint of spice. "Or maybe it's me," he said, and though his voice was low, she caught every word.

"That's kind of what I'm afraid of," she admitted.

He pulled himself upright. "Me?"

She shook her head." No. *Me*." She licked her lips and then jumped onboard the honesty train. "My reaction to you."

"Well, that doesn't sound so bad. But if it's truly scary, give me your hand and I'll help you through it."

She actually giggled—God, it was *definitely* the alcohol—and almost reached for him. Then she remembered that they were flirting in public, right there for the whole world to see. Her cheeks flamed, and she looked around the room, certain that everyone would be gawking. Or, worse, snapping pictures of the lusting couple and making fun of them all over the Internet.

Except that everyone was pretty much minding their own business. Even her friends had stopped gaping—all except for Hannah, who wasn't exactly gawking, but instead looked like she had Shelby's back. And when Hannah saw that Shel was looking, she grinned and flashed a thumbs-up sign.

So, okay. Apparently Shelby hadn't crossed the line to embarrassing herself or her friends.

"How long is your party going on?" he asked, apparently noticing the shift in her attention.

"Not much longer. It's a work night. We're all supposed to be in the office by nine." She pushed a stray curl behind her ear. "Well, some of us can get away with ten."

"Early, then," he said, with a smile she didn't understand. "My show *ends* at ten," he said, obviously noting her confusion. "It starts at six. So I'm usually in the studio by four-thirty to prep, though I can sometimes skate in at five and get away with it."

"That's right. You're a radio guy."

"You know my show?"

She shook her head quickly. *Mornings with Wood* sounded way too silly for her taste. Especially when she was still trying to slide into her day. "Brooke mentioned it."

"Ah."

Ridiculous, but he seemed disappointed.

"I mostly do podcasts," she said, as if to justify not listening to him. "Continuing education stuff." Which was about forty-six percent true. She also listened to classical, classic rock, and some country. But she streamed it from her phone specifically so she could avoid the irritating chatter of a DJ.

She winced, feeling guilty about the thought even though she knew Nolan couldn't read her mind.

"Something wrong?"

"It's just—I mean, it's already past eleven. Do you have a show in the morning?"

"I do." He shifted his stance, and when he spoke, his voice was the same—but different. A little lower. A little richer. But still laced with that same hint of amusement, as if he loved the way he looked at the world. *Join me, Nolan Wood, every weekday from six to ten on KIKX FM, 96.3 on your radio dial.*

She applauded, laughing. "That was awesome. You definitely have a radio voice."

He didn't exactly blush, but he looked pleased.

"So you have to be at work in about five hours?"

"Yup."

"But—"

"But why am I still talking to you instead of..."

"Instead of?"

The corner of his mouth quirked up. "Instead of buying you a coffee and sobering you up." He reached out, and gently brushed her lower lip with his forefinger, the connection making her body fire up all over again. "I want my good night kiss, after all."

A swarm of butterflies danced in her belly. And the truth was, she was already starting to get her wits back. Which wasn't necessarily a good thing, because all sorts of vintage Shelby doubts were creeping in as she imagined Nolan in here every night, his beautiful eyes searching the room until he found a woman to seduce with that wildly sensual voice. "You have this down to a science, don't you?"

A shadow crossed his eyes, and when he spoke, his voice had lost that lightness. "You'd be surprised how much I don't do this."

"Flirt with women?"

"Pursue a woman."

She shook her head, not understanding.

He took a step closer, gesturing between them. "I don't do this. I don't pursue. I don't usually have to."

"Oh." She studied his face, knowing it was probably a line. But there was an intensity in his eyes that surprised her. And despite common sense, she believed him.

"So how about it?" he asked.

She stiffened, her eyes wide, her whole body going hyper-aware. "It?" The word came out as a squeak.

"A coffee?"

"Oh." She relaxed a little. "I don't know. I mean, my friends…" She glanced over, and this time both Celia and Hannah were looking her direction—and waving her toward the door.

Nolan chucked. "If we're judging by peer pressure, I think I'm going to win. I'm not sure I've ever seen a group of friends so encouraging. Is that because of me or you?"

"Me," she said. "I told you, I don't usually…" She trailed off with a shrug.

"You don't usually drink coffee?" His voice rose in mock credulity. "Well, fine. I'll buy you some tea."

"I—" She'd intended to protest, but couldn't think of a reason why. "Just coffee, right?"

His smile reached his eyes. "Just coffee."

She nodded toward the front of the room. "I need to go tell my friends," she said, then hurried that direction.

"He is *so* hot," Hannah said, starting to rise with an obvious intent to hug.

"Don't you dare," Shelby said. "He's watching."

"We're all so proud of you," Hannah said, still seated. She pretended to dry a tear. "Our little girl's all grown up."

Shelby rolled her eyes and focused on Celia. "You really think it's okay? I mean, leaving with a strange guy?"

"Oh, please," Celia said. "He's Nolan Wood."

"Yeah, but—"

"Hang on." Celia lifted her hand to signal to one of the servers, and a pretty girl with wavy hair hurried over. "Hey, Tiffany," Celia said. "Question for you. That guy over there. Is he a regular? I mean, is he okay for..." She trailed off, glancing meaningfully at Shelby, who was pretty sure she was going to melt into the floor from embarrassment.

"Coffee," Shelby said. "We're just going for coffee."

"Uh-huh." Celia waved the comment away, her attention still on Tiffany.

"Nolan?" Tiffany said. "He's a regular, so I see him around here a lot." Her attention shifted to Shelby. "He's a nice guy. And he's friends with Reece and Brent, and I don't think they'd hang with an asshole."

Shelby started to ask who Reece and Brent were, then decided it didn't matter. Nolan had the earned his seal of approval. Which meant that now it was all on her.

She looked at her friends in panic.

"*Go*," Celia and Hannah said at the same time. "And tell us everything in the morning," Hannah added.

Shelby made a face. "Um, no. In the morning I'll be sober, and I really *won't* be talking about it."

"Maybe not," Hannah said, smiling wickedly. "But tonight, you're going to have one hell of a good time."

IT WASN'T until Nolan saw her start back toward him that he realized he'd been holding his breath. He exhaled, ridiculously relieved that he'd passed whatever test her friends had set for him.

Her. His dark-haired paradox. The woman who'd so unexpectedly grabbed him by the balls.

And, he realized with a start, he didn't even know her name.

"Nolan Sebastian Wood," he said, extending his hand as she returned.

"Um, yeah. I know. Well, not the Sebastian part. It suits you."

He kept his hand extended. "And you are?"

Her eyes went wide, and although she was clearly mortified that he didn't even know her name, he thought she looked absolutely adorable.

"Shelby," she finally said. "Shelby Drake." She slid her hand into his, a simple, polite gesture that shot through him like a goddamn rocket. He wanted to never let go—and at the same time he wanted his hands free so that he could explore every curvaceous, sensual inch of her. He wanted to lose himself in her—in this woman who'd managed to erase his shit day with nothing more than a few heat-filled looks, shy glances, and the sweetest smile he'd ever seen.

But first, he wanted to buy her a coffee.

"Halcyon's still open for a few more hours," he said, once they were standing on the sidewalk in front of The Fix. He ran through his mental Rolodex of which downtown coffee shops stayed open late. Frankly, there weren't many. "It's a short walk, and we can sip coffee and cook s'mores at the table. What do you say?"

"Um, sure."

"Not a fan of s'mores? Because I'm not even joking. There are little fire pits at each table, and—"

"You really want coffee?"

"Don't you?"

She licked her lips, and he realized that he didn't want coffee at all. He wanted that tongue in his mouth. Or other more interesting places.

He shifted, his jeans suddenly a bit too snug.

"It's just that—I, well…"

Even in the dark, he could see that her cheeks had turned bright red.

"I kind of thought that coffee was a euphemism," she whispered.

Oh, dear Lord, he was going to come right then.

"Where do you live?" he asked. "And where's your car?"

Conveniently, it turned out that she'd come with a friend. Even more conveniently, Nolan's car was only one block over. And best of all, she lived in Clarksville, a neighborhood right at the edge of downtown, in a rental just behind Sweetish Hill Bakery.

"This is cute," he said, after she'd fumbled her key into the lock and turned on the lights.

"If by cute you mean tiny, then yes it is." She turned in a circle, indicating the dollhouse-size house with its tidy, cozy living room with just enough room for a love seat, a recliner, and a television. Several hardback books were stacked neatly on the coffee table, including one called *Of Human Bondage*, which probably wasn't about what the name suggested. Her shoes fit perfectly into a small bench with cubbyholes by the door, and blankets filled baskets tucked into odd corners.

"There's also a kitchen and a bedroom," she continued, waving vaguely. "And that's pretty much it. I think it was a guesthouse for the house next door, but I don't have the history. I'm only renting." She shrugged. "It's big enough for me, and it's close to downtown. I work at a financial management company in the Frost Bank building. And, oh my God, I'm rambling, aren't I?"

She was, and although chatty women usually irritated him, he thought he could listen to her all night. "Do you have a coffee maker?" He *really* wanted her sober. To the point that he was on the verge of breaking his strict first date rule. Tipsy was fair, right? Because at the moment, tipsy seemed perfectly reasonable for a first kiss, first fuck, first everything.

Except, of course, it wasn't. He'd laid down strict rules for himself after Amanda had come to him in tears at the end of her second semester at UT. She'd gotten drunk, slept with a guy, and she'd been terrified that she was pregnant—or worse.

She hadn't been—thank God. But he'd been the one she'd turned to, begging him to keep her secret from their parents and their friends. Even from Jenna, to whom Amanda told everything. He'd seen her fear and her shame. She'd had her whole life planned out, and she was terrified that she'd knocked it off track because one stupid choice after a night of drinking.

And it wasn't even that she'd forgotten to use birth control. Even drunk, she'd insisted the guy wear a condom. And he had—but he'd been drunk, too, and, as Amanda had called it with rare humor under the circumstances, they'd suffered a "massive wardrobe failure."

"But it's not even that," Amanda had said. "I'm mad because it wasn't me. I mean, if I'd been with Dan," she continued, naming a previous boyfriend, "then drunk just makes it fun. But I didn't know this guy. So it was *this* talking." She pointed to the back of her head. "Some hormone center. But that's not me. And I didn't really want him. I mean, I didn't really know him."

They'd sat there in the Student Health Center as she shared her regrets and her fears. And even though she wasn't pregnant or infected, Nolan vowed right then and there to never, *ever*, sleep with a woman who was drunk, condom or not. He didn't want to risk hurting her. More than that, he wanted a woman in his bed to be there for *him*, not because her hormones were on overdrive.

He was almost thirty now, and over the years, he'd walked away from more than his share of tipsy women. But, dammit, he didn't want to walk away from Shelby. "A coffee maker," he repeated. "Do you have one?"

She blinked, then nodded. "Um, I have a Keurig."

"Great. Sit." He pointed to the couch. "Cream? Sugar?"

"In the fridge and by the machine. But I just take it black."

"You got it," he said, then disappeared into a kitchen that was, remarkably, even more organized and tidy than the living room. He found mugs organized by size and color in a cabinet above the Keurig machine. A rack of pods sat beside it, and he selected Columbian for her, figuring that would be stronger than the Hazelnut. And decaf was completely out of the question.

He didn't bother making one for himself, and as soon as the machine stopped sputtering, he grabbed the mug and carried it carefully back into the living room, only to find Shelby on the gray couch, her head back and her eyes closed, a bright green pillow clutched to her chest.

Well, hell.

"Here," he said gently. He considered offering to help her into bed, but decided the risk was too high. Once in her bedroom, he wasn't sure he'd have the strength to leave unless she kicked him out. And he was pretty damn sure she wasn't going to do that.

"Coffee," he said, bending to put it on the coffee table. She opened her eyes—green now, but hadn't they been blue in the bar?—and smiled so sweetly that a lump rose in his throat.

Don't sit. You'll only want to stay.

"Thank you," she said, then scooted over to make room for him before reaching for the coffee and taking a sip.

He shook his head. "I should go."

Her eyes widened behind the rim of the mug. She swallowed, then shook her head. "Wait. What?"

He moved a few steps toward the door, not wanting to lose his resolve.

Immediately, she was on her feet, the coffee on one of her stone coasters. "But—I thought. I mean, we—"

"What?" he said, then wanted to kick himself. He knew damn well *what*. He was just stalling because he didn't want to leave.

Her throat moved as she swallowed, and he saw courage flash in those fascinating eyes that now seemed greenish-gray. "It's just that I've never brought a guy home before."

Something like pride swelled in him, and he tamped it down. He really didn't need his damn ego hijacking the situation. "Technically, I brought you home."

She took another step toward him. "But aren't we—"

She cut herself off, her cheeks pink. "I just meant I wanted … oh, *hell*," she said, then leaned forward and captured his mouth in a kiss so unexpected and so delicious that when she finally broke the kiss, he kept hold of her arm out of the irrational fear that if he let her go, she might vanish like some magical creature.

With his hand clutching her arm, he drew in a breath to steady himself, all of his energy concentrated on not yanking her toward him for another, deeper kiss. "Is that what you wanted?" he asked.

She shook her head, her eyes never leaving his. And though she never wavered, he knew that she was calling on all her courage to make this moment happen. "No," she said. "I want more."

He considered his options—considered his rules— and then he said the only truth he knew. "So do I."

"Nolan—"

He pressed a finger to her lips to silence her and made his choice. "Close your eyes, Shelby. Just close your eyes."

Chapter Six

SHELBY BREATHED IN DEEP, her eyes closed, her body humming. Her lips were parted, and a sweet anticipation filled her, heating her blood and making her hyperaware of everything around her. The slight breeze from her ceiling fan. The low rumble of late-night traffic. The soft scrape of the miniature palm tree against the screen of her window.

Most of all, she was aware of Nolan. She couldn't see him, but she sensed him. Right there, his eyes on her. And, soon, his lips. His hands. His everything.

She still didn't know what had gotten into her, but she wanted this. His touch, his kiss. All of it.

She felt the shift in the air and heard the soft pad of his shoes on her carpet. "That's good, Shelby. Now I want you do something for me." She nodded. Right then she was willing to do pretty much anything. "Touch your nose."

Her eyes flew open. "What?"

His mouth tilted sideways. "I told you, baby. I want you sober. Close your eyes and touch your nose."

"I'm totally sober," she protested. "Two, three, five, seven, eleven, thirteen, seventeen, nineteen, twenty-three, twenty-ni—hey!"

He had her by the wrist, and his expression could only be described as baffled. "What on earth are you doing?"

"Prime numbers all the way to a hundred." She tugged her wrist free and put her hands on her hips. "I bet *you* can't do them drunk."

"I can't even do them sober. Just touch your nose."

She frowned, but closed her eyes. The trouble was, she could recite prime numbers in her sleep. Drunk. Sober. Anesthetized. But what if she missed her nose? She didn't think she was drunk. Maybe back in the bar, but she felt fine now. But if she was wrong…

She opened her eyes, grabbed the mug, and took a long swallow, ignoring the way he laughed at her. She put the mug back, stood up, and took a long, deep breath.

Then she closed her eyes, thrust out her free hand, and before she could talk herself out of trying, brought the tip of her finger right smack against the end of her nose.

"There," she said triumphantly, opening her eyes and smiling at him. "Now kiss me, dammit."

And, thank God, he did, moving closer to slide his

hand around to cup the nape of her neck. Then he tilted her head back so that when he bent down, his mouth fit perfectly over hers, and the intensity of the electrical connection that arced between them rocked her to her core.

They touched only at lips and hands, and yet it felt as if they were connected at every possible point.

"You taste so good," he said. "I don't ever want to stop kissing you."

"Then don't." She was fine with that plan. Forever kisses seemed perfectly reasonable under the circumstances.

But then his other hand joined the party, skimming down the skintight dress and finding her nipple, stiff under the stretchy black material. A new kind of shock shimmied through her, and she revised her position on kisses. They were fine as part of the meal, but she didn't want to stick to just one item.

"Come here," he said, then tugged her to the love seat. He nodded to the book on top of the stack. "Any tips for us in there?" he asked, his mouth curved into a tease.

She followed the direction of his gaze and saw that he was looking at *Of Human Bondage*. "Definitely not," she said. "It's a classic. Have you read it?"

"I'm more a graphic novel sort of guy," he said, lifting her up and settling her on his lap so that she straddled his hips, making it impossible for her to ignore the fact that he was clearly having at least as good a time as she was.

"Oh," she said.

"Yeah," he said, in a tone that suggested he thought her little sound of surprise was in response to his comment about graphic novels, when it was actually about his cock. "Do you read them?"

"Never have." Should she continue this conversation or tell him to shut up and kiss her again? Did he think she wanted to talk because she was nervous?

"Start with *Watchmen*," he said, and as he spoke, his fingers traced her collarbone and her shoulder, starting a fresh round of magic in her body and making her nipples harden painfully. "It's my favorite."

He bent forward and pressed his lips to her shoulder, right where it still burned from the heat of his finger.

"Okay," she agreed, melting beneath the heat of his mouth—then melting even more when he trailed his kisses down, finally closing his mouth over her breast, still covered by the thin material of the little black dress.

He teased her breast with his mouth. His tongue tracing the v-neck before his teeth grazed her nipple through the material. At the same time, his hand was still holding the base of the neck, ensuring that she arched back enough to give him access but not so much it felt as though she was falling.

His other hand was busy on her thigh, slowly inching higher and higher.

"Nolan," she gasped, the onslaught of his attentions making her wild. With both legs straddling him, the material of her dress had been pushed up to her hips. Now she was wide open and vulnerable. She didn't feel shy, though. On the contrary, she rocked her hips, wanting to feel his erection hard beneath her.

She was so incredibly wet, a fact he discovered as his finger explored the soft skin of her inner thigh, slick with the evidence of how very much she wanted him. "I like that," he said, with such raw honestly she felt her sex clench and wished that he was inside her.

"Please," she begged as he slid his finger under her panties then teased her core. "Please," she repeated as the fingers at the nape of her neck moved to her cleavage, stretching the material until a breast popped out, and Nolan's mouth closed over it like a man who was starving.

His teeth tightened on her nipple, and she arched back, crying out as two fingers thrust inside her core at the same time that he sucked on her breast, sending an arc of electricity racing between her sex and her tit and taking her so close to an orgasm she wanted to weep.

Shamelessly, she writhed against him, trying to finish herself, but he nipped at her earlobe and whispered, "None of that."

"Then fuck me. Please, Nolan, I want you inside me."

"Christ, baby, I thought you'd never ask."

He unfastened his jeans as she started to rise enough to get out of her panties. "No, leave them on. Just pull them aside. Trust me," he added in response to what must have been a look of confusion on her part.

"Condom?" she asked, relieved when he pulled out a wallet and then sheathed himself.

"Fast or slow?" he asked with a playful grin.

"Both," she said, and then before he could take charge, she positioned herself over him, and in one hard thrust downward, impaled herself on him, crying out both because he was big, and also because she was wet and ready enough that it felt so ridiculously good.

"That was the fast," she said as he laughed and pulled her in for a kiss. "You'll have to help with the slow."

He understood what she meant, and he took her hips in his hands, helping keep a steady motion as she rose up and down, riding his cock as the intensity built and built between them.

"I'm so close, baby. Can you come for me?"

She shook her head, and he released one hand, moving it to cup her, his finger teasing her clit as she continued to ride, more frantically now that she could feel the explosion rising in her.

"Now," she cried, as she felt his body start to release. And as if she'd made it happen, every cell in her body seemed to shatter in an explosion of pure, white stardust.

Her core tightened around his cock, taking him even further, and when they were both spent, he shifted on the small sofa so that she could collapse on top of him.

His eyes were closed, but he opened them to kiss her. Then said simply, "Wow."

She could only nod agreement, and then she put her head on his shoulder and fell into a warm, blissful sleep.

THEY WOKE ONCE during the night, and Nolan carried her to the bed, then climbed in beside her, something he never did. Usually, he bolted as fast as he could. But there was something about this woman that called to him. That clicked with him. And when she opened her eyes and sleepily said, "What?" he told her that he wanted to make love to her again since he'd have to go to work before she woke up in the morning.

She nodded with an eager smile, and they made love slowly and sweetly before falling asleep again, twined in each other's arms.

He woke at four-fifteen when Connor texted to

ask where the fuck he was. Nolan bolted out of bed and yanked on his clothes. As he headed toward her front door, his body shook from the force of a massive yawn, and he was struck by the realization of how little sleep he'd had.

With a self-satisfied grin, he backtracked to her kitchen, then selected a travel mug from the neat row in her cabinet. He hoped she didn't mind, and he was grateful for the excuse to see her again and return it. He drummed his fingers on the counter as he waited for the machine to finish brewing, then added some cream to cool it off. Then he was on his way again, shutting the door firmly behind him and double-checking to make sure it locked.

The station was in north Austin on the I-35 access road, but he didn't have to worry about traffic at this time of the morning, and he rolled into the booth at five after five.

"What the hell?" Connor began, but Nolan just held up a hand.

"Hot date," he said, with a grin and an eyebrow waggle.

Connor just shook his head and handed Nolan a binder. "Sponsor information. Manny emailed it to me last night. He wants you to read through, and try to work a few references into your schtick. Apparently ad revenue is dropping so we're trying to set ourselves apart from the other stations. Be more organic with our product placement."

"Great." Nolan flipped through the text-filled pages of the binder with distaste, his stomach twisting into knots as he thought about having to read through the whole damn thing.

"Here."

Nolan looked up in time to catch the USB flash drive that Connor tossed his way. "I went through and dictated some highlights of the first five sponsors. Just a quick and dirty run-through, but I figured it would give you material for today. Should take you ten minutes to listen to."

"Yeah?" Nolan stared at the drive. "Thanks."

Connor lifted a shoulder, suggesting it was no big deal. "I figure you've got better things to do than waste your time reading through that tome."

"Damn right," Nolan said, clutching the flash drive like a lifeline. Nolan hadn't told Connor he was dyslexic. Hell, he'd never told anyone except Amanda and the folks at the Dyslexia Reading & Tutoring Room, a nonprofit organization focused on helping kids with dyslexia learn decoding and other skills to help with both reading and self-esteem.

He'd been quietly working with the organization for years, but while he didn't keep his involvement a secret, he also didn't advertise it.

Maybe Connor had simply realized that it took Nolan forever to work his way through a pile of papers. All Nolan knew for sure was that Connor hadn't complained when Nolan asked him to summarize the daily news. And whenever Manny dumped a lot of reading on him, Connor always said it was the producer's job to keep the talent's slate clean.

He shot a glance toward Connor as he plugged in the drive, but he didn't ask. Better not to know. It wasn't like Nolan wanted to talk about it. He just wanted to do his job. And think about Shelby.

And when six o'clock rolled around, that's exactly what he did. "Gooooooood morning, Austin! It's Thursday morning, and this is *Mornings with Wood*. And, yeah, it's one of those days where that show's title is pretty damn appropriate. Welcome, listeners, to my new favorite day. Yeah, that's right, I got me a little somethin' somethin' last night, and I'm bouncing off the walls with all the good vibes."

He hit the button on the console, and the sexy female voice crooned, "Oooooh, Nolan. Tell me more."

"Now, you know a gentleman never kisses and tells, but maybe this will give you a hint. Back with the morning traffic after a little AC/DC."

As he finished his riff, he faded into *Shook Me All Night Long*, then sat back in his chair, shot Connor a self-satisfied grin, then spent the next three minutes and thirty-two seconds lost in some damn sweet memories.

Chapter Seven

THE SHARP BUZZ of her cell phone interrupted Shelby's NSFW dream. Still half asleep and smiling, she groped for it, accepted the call without paying attention to the screen, and murmured, "Nolan."

"What?"

Alan.

She was upright and wide awake in an instant, the sheet gathered around her hips, revealing how very naked she was. She yanked it up and covered her breasts.

"What did you say?"

"I said Alan," she lied. "Sorry, I was asleep. What did you think I said?" *Idiot.* She banged the heel of her hand against her forehead, then looked around her bedroom, but all signs of the man whose name she'd really spoken were gone. For a moment, disappointment warred with mortification in her belly.

Then she remembered that he'd warned her he'd be leaving before she woke.

Which meant he hadn't walked out without a trace.

Which was good for her ego.

On the whole, though, it really didn't much matter. He hadn't suggested they go out again, and they'd made no plans to see each other after work or on the weekend. And why would they? He was a local celebrity, after all. He was probably booked with a different woman every night from here to eternity.

And that was just fine by her. Because while Nolan Wood might have been a fun diversion—a *very* fun diversion—he didn't fit into her life plan at all. He was a guy whose show title was a double entendre, and whose drive-time program was known for being raucous and racy.

So, no. He just didn't fit. Not like the man on the other end of the phone line did.

"I woke you?" Alan chuckled. "You and the girls must have had one hell of a time at that bachelorette party."

"Oh, well, yeah. You could say that." She felt the slow burn of embarrassment creep over her body. "Wait. What time is it?"

"Almost nine."

"*Ack.* I need to get out of here." She leapt out of bed, then looked immediately around for her robe since she was naked and talking to Alan. She couldn't find it. "Listen, I need to go. Can we talk later?"

"Sure, sure. I only called to remind you about tomorrow. Dinner at your parents."

"With the dean of the department," she said. "I remember. Meet you there?"

"Don't be ridiculous. I'll pick you up at six."

She smiled as they ended the call. Alan had impeccable manners, and they always had a lovely time when her parents put on a faculty event. It was sure to be an absolutely wonderful evening. The kind she inevitably enjoyed, with lots of interesting conversation about the kind of theoretical mathematics she found fascinating but didn't need to keep up with in her job.

She showered and dressed quickly, ignoring Hannah's crumpled dress on the floor of the bathroom—then hurried to the office, hitting every red light on the way.

She was already up the elevator and through the reception doors when she got Hannah's text. *Where R U?*

Frowning, Shelby tapped out a reply, hoping there wasn't a crisis brewing. *Lobby. Overslept. Tell me F's not looking for me.*

F was Frank Talbot, Shelby's immediate superior. And the one who'd trained her to always get to the office by eight so that she had time to get herself organized before the day began in earnest.

Just hurry.

Shelby sighed, but picked up her pace, wondering what kind of crisis had landed on her desk. Major, if Hannah knew about it, since that meant the legal department was involved. *Shit.* She trotted the rest of the way, thankful to be back in her comfortable, sensible shoes.

"What's going on?" she asked, bursting through her office door and finding Celia, Hannah, Leslie, Kayla, and Ria huddled around her desk.

"Girl, what did you *do* last night," Kayla asked. A stunning black woman, Kayla wore her hair so short you could see her scalp, a style that accentuated her huge eyes—which right now seemed even bigger than normal as she stared down Shelby with what looked like a mixture of surprise and respect.

Ria giggled. She was sitting on the edge of Shelby's desk, her swinging feet decked out in two inch platforms sporting four inch heels. At four foot three, Ria was always trying to compensate. "I think the question is what *didn't* she do."

"I know, right?" Hannah said. "I swear, my little girl's all grown up. I'm so proud."

All five women laughed at that, but Shelby continued to stand in front of her desk, her mind spinning. "So this has nothing to do with Frank?"

"Shut the door," Hannah said, even though she was moving to shut it herself. "Go ahead," she said to

Celia, who hit a button on her phone and put it in the middle of the desk.

"They have an app," Celia explained.

"Who?" Shelby asked.

"The show streams live in audio," she continued, not answering Shel. "Sometimes there's even video," she added, as if they were just discussing the weather.

"It's really funny," Kayla added, her tone apologetic as the last strains of Heart's *Crazy On You* faded out. "I mean, he's good on the air, and it's not like he ever calls you by name."

Oh, God. Shelby trepidation ramped up until it hovered somewhere near terrified. And when Hannah pushed one of the guest chairs up behind her, she sat without question.

"Aaaand we're back!" Nolan's voice filled the room, and even though Shelby was already five thousand percent sure that she wasn't going to like what he was going to say, she couldn't deny the effect that smooth, sensual voice was having on her body—or the decadent memories that rushed to fill her mind.

Casually, she crossed her legs, then clasped her hands on her knees as she breathed deliberately through her nose.

"We've got time for one more request. Remember, folks, after one night, I can't say if she rocked my world, but she definitely rocked *me*. So that's our theme. So you say it, and if I play it, you get two tickets to the upcoming Pink Chameleon concert in

San Antonio—all because I'm in one hell of a good mood today."

"Ooooh, Nolan. Tell me more!"

"Ah-ah-ah. Believe me. It's way too *hard* to describe how I feel. But then again, maybe that's why we call the show *Mornings with Wood*. Hey, there, caller. What's your name?"

He was talking about her. The simple reality slammed into her mind as Nolan went back and forth with some guy named Tommy. He was actually talking about *her.* On the radio.

Not only that, but he was talking about her *and* about hard-ons *on the freaking radio.*

"The bastard," she said as she snatched up Celia's phone. "I can just push this little phone icon to call into the show?" she asked, inspecting the screen.

"Are you nuts?" Hannah said. "What are you going to say?"

"I'm going to tell him to stop." Had she told him it was okay to do this? Last night, when she'd joked about their sex being too hot for the radio, had he really thought she meant that this—*this*—was okay?

"You can't call in," Leslie said. "Someone will recognize your voice."

"Shit." She tossed the phone back on the desk, the cringed at Celia's perturbed, "Hey!"

"Sorry." She drew in a breath and tried to calm herself, but that really wasn't happening. "It doesn't matter if I call in. Everyone already knows. What the *hell* is he doing? Everyone in that whole damn bar knows it's me."

"No, no," Ria said. "Just us, and we wouldn't tell a soul."

"You never go to The Fix," Hannah added. "No one knows your name."

"And even if the staff knew, they wouldn't say," Leslie assured her.

Shelby looked to Kayla, who shrugged. "I don't know. I mean, I *doubt* anybody knows."

"I could call the studio," Shelby said. "I mean, the office. So I'm not on the air."

Hannah leaned against the side of the desk. "If you really want to talk to him about this, then call him at home."

Shelby licked her lips. "I don't have his number."

She watched as the five women exchanged pointed glances.

"Well," Hannah said slowly, "then my guess is that this is just a riff on his part. Tomorrow, he'll be on to something else, and no one will even remember today."

"Oh." Shelby said, and despite the fact that she'd already told herself that this thing with Nolan was a non-starter … and despite the fact that his ridiculous on-air announcement *really* capped that sentiment … the stark realization that she'd had a one-night stand without even realizing it hit her hard.

A one-night stand with a man who'd made her

feel things she didn't know she could feel, and want things she didn't know she could want. Who'd had her begging and laughing. Who'd hands-down shared the best sexual experience of her life. And then he'd gone and used their sexual exploits as fodder for his radio program. The whole thing made her queasy. "This is a nightmare," she whispered. "I mean, it's a nightmare of absolute epic proportions."

"Oh, hell," Leslie said, glancing at her watch. "I've got an interview in ten minutes. Honey, it'll be fine." She gave Shelby a squeeze on the shoulder as she headed toward the door.

Shelby bent to put her head between her knees as Celia paused the program. "Oh, God. What if Alan hears? What if my parents hear? What if Frank hears?"

"Hears what?" The familiar deep voice of her boss came from behind her, and she almost jumped to her feet, but was forced to keep her head down by Hannah's firm hand on her back.

"That she has some sort of horrible intestinal bug," Hannah said. "Her doctor says it's not contagious, so she came in. But the cramps and the, you know, bathroom runs…" She trailed off, her voice reflecting disgust and sympathy. "I told her she should call in, but she's so damn responsible."

"Well, for heaven's sake, Shelby. Do you really feel that bad?"

"Yes, sir," she said, which wasn't exactly a lie.

"You're not working retail, you know. You're a professional. You can make your own schedule. Have your assistant move your appointments and go home."

"Right. I should. I will. Thank you."

She kept her head down until she heard the door latch behind her, then rose up. "You are an incredible liar. And I'm still completely screwed."

"No, you're not," Hannah said firmly.

"Unless she's talking about last night," Kayla said, and they all burst into laughter. Even Shelby, who figured that this must be some form of gallows humor. Because, really, this situation was so not good.

So. Absolutely. Freaking. Totally. Not. Good.

The radio. He talked about her—he talked about her and sex—on his radio program.

That simple truth ran through her head over and over as she headed home, as she made herself a pot of coffee and some slice-and-bake cookies, and as she settled on her couch to watch mindless television.

After a few hours, though, she clicked off the TV, realizing that mindless television was too mindless to block out the murderous—and unfortunately still lustful—thoughts of Nolan. After all, this very couch had been the background of what was now a ridiculously pleasant memory. At least it had been until his stupid radio stunt had tainted it.

"Well, hell," she muttered, then picked up *The Man Who Knew Infinity*, a biography of a self-taught mathematical genius that she'd started a few nights before. If anything could take her mind off Nolan, it was math, and after half an hour, that theory proved to be true. She'd become completely absorbed in the beauty of the story—so much so that she jumped when she heard the sharp knock at her door.

"Shelby? It's Nolan."

She froze. Just completely froze right there on her couch. Then she realized that the blinds were drawn, and there was no way he could see her. So she carefully put her book down and moved to stand next to the door.

She wasn't sure why she did that—she had no intention of talking to him or opening the door, mostly because she didn't know what she wanted to say. He'd left her no room for planning or rehearsal. But, strangely, she'd been drawn closer. And so now she stood just inches away, her palm pressed lightly to the wood.

"Hello? Well, shit. Your car's here, Shelby. I don't have your number, so I couldn't call, but I know you're there. Except maybe she's not," he added, his voice changing slightly, as if he was a voice actor playing two roles. "Maybe she's taking a walk or going on a bike ride. Or maybe she's with a friend. Hell, maybe she's in some other man's bed, in which case, I just might have to kill him. *Shelby*."

Her name, accompanied by the sharp ring of her

doorbell made her jump and clap her hand over her mouth.

"I have your travelers mug. If you don't open the door, I'm holding it for ransom!" A pause, then the second voice, "She's not there, you idiot. Leave the mug, and go."

She put her hand on the knob, and almost—*almost* —turned it. But then she chickened out and simply stood there and listened to the lid of her mailbox squeaking. The clatter of the mug hitting bottom. The patter of his footsteps on the stairs.

And when, finally, she heard the purr of his Audi's engine pulling away, she sank to the ground, leaned her back against the door, and sobbed as the tears she'd been holding back all day flooded out in earnest.

Chapter Eight

NOLAN SHOULD NEVER HAVE TOLD Connor any of it. But, dammit, he'd never been this flummoxed by a woman. "We went out," he'd said to his friend that morning, before the show got underway. "We had a great time. And now, crickets. I even left my card inside the coffee mug I returned. But no email, no text, no call, no anything."

"Baffling," Connor had said dryly.

"What?"

"Oh, come on, Nolan. Have so many women been chasing you that you forgot that some women aren't celebrity chasers? Maybe she didn't want her life blasted across the airwaves."

"My entire life is a goddamn morning show," Nolan had said. "It's just a routine. And she was anonymous."

"But it's not her routine," Connor had replied. "And it wasn't anonymous to her."

"Oh, fuck you," Nolan had retorted, because he hated when his friend was right. But he didn't riff on the date at all. Instead, he played Simon & Garfunkel's *The Sound of Silence* without commentary. Just because.

By the time the show ended, he wanted to bang his head against a wall. He'd been off the entire morning, his energy sucked down a well drilled by Connor's words.

The worst of it was that he was filling in tomorrow because Wayne, the usual Saturday morning host, was on vacation. Which meant he had one more day of fumbling like an idiot on the airwaves instead of chilling and getting his mojo back.

Well, hell.

He considered getting a second opinion from Amanda, but he didn't need it. Connor was right. Nolan had been living in his little bubble of bliss, and —just like he did with everything—he blew it out across the airwaves.

But, goddammit, he wanted to see her again. Which meant that somehow, he had to make this right.

He waited until five-thirty, hoping she'd be home from work, then drove to her house. Once again, her car was in the drive. And, once again, he climbed the steps. Two quick knocks, and then he waited on the porch, shifting his weight from foot to foot even as he told himself that he was wasting his time, because she wasn't going to open the damn door.

But then he felt the vibrations on the porch as someone inside the house hurried across the living room for the door. He heard her call, "You're early! Hang on!" And he held his breath as the latch clicked and she pulled the door open.

"You said six—*oh!* Nolan."

He saw her move to shut the door, and took a step forward. "I'm sorry. Please, don't slam the door."

"I wasn't going to," she said, but she stood in the doorway and blocked the entrance, so she clearly had no intention of letting him in, either.

"You look nice," he said, which was true. But she also looked different enough that if he'd seen her on the street, he might not have recognized her. She wore a tailored gray suit and a white button-down shirt. Her shoes had closed toes, low-heels, and resembled something his mom might wear to church. She was wearing stockings, but he had a feeling they were of the pantyhose variety, and that there was no sexy garter hidden under the trim skirt.

Inexplicably, just the sight of her in that buttoned-up outfit made him want to pull her close and kiss her hard.

"What do you want, Nolan?"

"What? Oh, I told you. I wanted to say that I'm sorry. I shouldn't have blasted all that about us on the radio. I was—it's just that I don't have much of a filter when I'm doing my show. That's the schtick that keeps the ratings up. But I should have considered your feelings."

"That's a really nice apology," she said. "Thank you."

"Yeah?" He grinned. That had been remarkably easy. "Listen, I'm about to go get a bite. Want to join me?"

"Oh." She licked lips that he desperately wanted to kiss. Maybe they could order in…

"Um," she said, not quite meeting his eyes. "I really can't." She looked up, her expression pleading. "I had a great time on Wednesday. Really. And I really do accept your apology. But that girl from Wednesday—she wasn't really me."

"Aliens? Pod people? Clones?"

She rolled her eyes. "I was wasted."

He stepped forward, and since she held her ground and continued to block the entrance, they were only inches from each other. Awareness crackled between them, and from the cornered, desperate look in her eye, he was certain he wasn't the only one who felt it. "You weren't wasted," he said simply. "We worked pretty damn hard to establish that."

"I was overwhelmed," she amended.

"I have that effect."

"Look, Nolan. Please, just go."

"Come on, Shelby. We had a good time together. Let's grab some dinner and just talk this time."

"I—I—"

"What?"

"I'm seeing someone," she blurted. "His name's Alan. He's a professor."

"Oh." For a moment, he couldn't think of anything to say, and he realized that her little confession hit him harder than he'd like.

"I know I shouldn't have—I mean, at the bar—but I really *was* wasted at first. And I really did have a good time with you, but I never meant to start something, and I didn't think that you did either, and—" She cut herself off abruptly, as if she'd simply run out of words.

Nolan considered making it easy on her and simply walking away. Except that wouldn't be easy on him. And maybe he was making excuses, but he'd held her in his arms. He'd felt her body tremble around his. Maybe she did have a boyfriend, but she wanted Nolan. He was certain of it.

So he stayed, and he looked pointedly at her left hand, and then back up at her eyes. "I don't see a ring. And I don't see your guy."

"I—well, no. So?"

He lifted his brows and flashed a wide, wicked grin. "All's fair in love and war."

"This isn't about love or war."

"All's fair in sex and sin. Better?"

Her lips twitched, but she got herself under control and shook her head. "Listen, Nolan. We're not really ... compatible."

He reached out, then twirled a strand of her hair around his finger before gently tracing her jawline. "Aren't we?" She trembled under his touch, and a sweet shot of victory raced through his veins.

She drew a noisy breath. "I'll admit a bit of a weakness for you, but that's only because I don't really date that much and you—"

"Fascinated you? Titillated you? Aroused you?"

"Unnerved me," she said firmly.

"Yeah?" He flashed his best seductive smile. "I'm happy to unnerve you again."

"Please. I have a date, and you need to go."

A date? He turned, then saw a Lexus turn onto her street.

"Please," she said, a note of panic in her voice.

"All right," he said, then paused at her steps to turn back. "But just so you know, Ben Franklin is my personal hero."

Her brow furrowed as she shook her head in confusion. "What are you talking about?"

"If at first you don't succeed..." He trailed off with a shrug. "Call it fair warning."

She rolled her eyes. "Benjamin Franklin never said that."

Nolan frowned, then pointed at her. "Maybe not," he conceded. "But he should have."

SHELBY STOOD by the front door of her parents' house, her hand clasped in Alan's as they said goodnight to the small group of faculty members who'd come over for the evening.

"This man is going places." The dean clapped his hand on Alan's shoulder as he smiled at Shelby. "He's a good one."

"I know," she said, forcing a smile. Usually she loved faculty dinners at her parents' house, but tonight had bordered on painful. It was Nolan's fault, of course. His promise—no, *threat*—that he wasn't going away. And, honestly, she didn't need that kind of complication in her well-ordered life.

She sighed as she closed the door behind the last guest, feeling like a walking, talking lesson in not breaking your own rules.

"Something wrong?" Alan asked, as he stroked her cheek, his brown eyes dark with worry.

"I'll second Alan's question," her mother said. "You were very quiet tonight." She was a tall woman with the build of a ballerina. She tended to wear her hair up except when she was home alone, and the style only made the resemblance more apparent. Now, she pulled out the pins and let her dark hair fall around her shoulders. It was the only feature they had in common, and Shelby was grateful to have inherited her mom's lovely hair.

"It's nothing," she assured them, leaning up against her father's broad chest and relaxing into his hug. "Just some stuff going on at work."

"Trouble?" her mother asked. "Because you need to keep in mind that corporate policy and rules are in place for a reason. Just like the rules of academia. You follow them, you climb the ladder, and once you're at the top, the view is much clearer. Right now, your view is blocked by everyone else trying to climb up with you."

"I know, Mom." She appreciated her parent's work ethic and their tenacity. But the advice really didn't apply. Not that she intended to share the real issue with her mother. Not ever. But certainly not with Alan around. "It's just a snafu with an audit," she lied. "The client didn't turn over some information and he's made his life horribly messy—and mine along with it."

That was true enough. But as she already had a plan for dealing with the Thompson audit, that wasn't what was weighing on her mind.

"You'll work it out," Alan said, tilting her chin up and stealing a kiss. "You're too good not to."

"Thanks." She relaxed against his long, lean body, breathing deep and remembering that this was exactly what she wanted. A man to support and understand her. A home where real problems were handled, not joked about, and things were discussed in private, not on the damn airwaves.

"Hey," Alan said, loosening her arms. "Love the affection, but I'm also a fan of breathing."

"Sorry," she said, forcing a smile. "I got carried away." *Wasn't that the truth?*

"You're sure you're not upset with me?" Alan asked, as they all made their way to the kitchen-dining area, where Shelby loaded the dishwasher as Alan cleared.

"You mean about tomorrow? Don't be silly."

Alan had learned only that morning that the department expected him to give a speech next week to visiting faculty from three foreign universities. And even though they were supposed to go to Celia's wedding together on Saturday, she'd assured him that she had no problems going alone if he needed to use that time to prepare for such a big opportunity.

"I know how tight your schedule is. And I'm more than capable of eating wedding cake and sitting with my friends all by myself."

"And you want to do your best," her father said, passing Alan a glass of port. "We're very proud of you." He gave Shelby and her mother a drink, too, and they all toasted Alan's success.

"What about you, sugar?" her dad asked. "When will we see you make partner?"

"I don't know," she admitted. "I know Frank's rooting for me, but the partners won't offer me even a junior partnership until I've handled a larger corporate account." She already did consulting work for a number of small corporations, often with only one or two employees. It was great training, but if she wanted to be a partner, she needed the experience she'd get from a long-term project doing in-depth consulting with a large local or nationwide company.

Since she *did* want to be a partner, that was something she talked with Frank about on a regular basis. And she knew he was keeping his eyes open, watching the client list with an eye to assigning her a partnership-track project. "The company's doing a lot of outreach right now, so new clients are flooding in. I'm crossing my fingers I get a new assignment soon."

"You could always teach," Alan said later, after they'd said goodbye to her parents and were back in Shelby's living room. "We could work side by side. And someday we could host faculty parties like your parents."

She looked up at him, surprised. She'd always assumed they were on the same wavelength about the future, but just as they'd never talked about being exclusive, they'd also never talked about settling down.

"I don't think I want to teach," she said, sidestepping that particular elephant in the room. "I like getting my hands dirty."

"Do you? Well, maybe we can get dirty together." He pulled her into his arms, and she waited for a sensual tingle that flat-out didn't come. "We could sweep the kitchen. Wash the dishes. Or we could get dirty in other, more interesting ways."

He brushed a kiss over her lips, but she pulled back, smiling in a way that she hoped didn't look forced. "Could I take a rain check? I'm really tired, and my head's been hurting ever since I drank that port."

Most of all, I don't want to sleep with you.

The bare truth washed over her, both scaring and saddening her. Because this was Alan. Her perfect guy. The guy who satisfied all of her checkboxes. And he was talking sex and suggesting a home together.

She should be turning cartwheels.

But she wasn't.

Her whole life, she'd known how she wanted her future to look. So why was it that lately her vision had skewed?

Chapter Nine

"TURN ON 96.3," Hannah said, shoving through Shelby's front door with both hands full of dresses on hangers and a duffel bag swung over each shoulder. "Your boyfriend's on the air."

"He does weekdays, and he's not my boyfriend," Shelby said, taking a handful of dresses and spreading them over the back of the couch. "I only need to borrow one. For that matter, I'm sure I already own something that's just fine for a wedding."

"A, I'm sure you don't. And B, he's subbing for Wayne Dorsey."

"Who is…?"

"On vacation, apparently. And the Saturday morning DJ."

Since Shelby had made no move to tune in, Hannah plugged her own phone into Shelby's small set of speakers and opened up the streaming app. The one that Shelby had very sternly talked herself out of downloading last night after a long hot shower and two glasses of Chardonnay.

There was a crackle of static, and then the last verse of The Rolling Stones' *(I Can't Get No) Satisfaction* filled the room.

Hannah tilted her head toward the speakers. "Got something to confess?"

"I have no idea what you're talking about," Shelby said.

"Mmm." Hannah pulled out a long, slinky red dress and held it up in front of Shelby.

"I'm not wearing red to a wedding."

Hannah made a face. "Good point. But it's loose on me. You should try it on."

Shelby tilted her head. "I don't want to climb in and out of your wardrobe. I only need one dress. And why do you have so many cocktail and evening dresses anyway? I know you aren't off doing weekly galas because half of these still have tags."

Hannah lifted her chin, looking a little defensive. "I found a few online discount stores I really like. Besides, if I weren't a mobile closet, you'd be out of luck."

"That one," Shelby said, deciding it was time to change the subject. The dress was cerulean blue, with a halter-style top, a full skirt, and a built-in petticoat.

"Good choice," Hannah said. "I'm impressed."

"Just because I dress professionally at work doesn't mean I want to wear sackcloth to a wedding."

"I know." Hannah winked. "It's just so much fun to tease you."

She passed Shelby the dress just as the song ended, and Shelby's breath caught in her throat as Nolan's voice filtered out from the speakers. "But I tried," he said, his voice singsong. "And in the end, I got bupkis. So I ask you folks, is she playing hard to get? Or am I just hard-headed? We'll do a little psychoanalysis of me, Nolan Wood standing in for Wayne Dorsey on Sunny-side Saturday, right after this message from our sponsor."

Hannah crossed her arms and stared Shelby down as an ad for a local pet store started.

"Fine," Shelby said when Hannah's stare started to get creepy. "He came over yesterday."

"And?"

"And nothing," Shelby admitted. "I told him I had a date and sent him away." She cringed a little, then confessed. "He came by the day before, and I pretended I wasn't home."

"You're kidding, right?"

"Sadly, no. Apparently, at heart, I'm an eleven-year-old girl."

"Well, thirteen, maybe. Tops." Hannah exhaled, the sound weirdly maternal. Then she sat on the edge of the couch, crunching at least five dress skirts in the process. "Okay, let's analyze this. Do you like him?"

"Yeah," Shelby said honestly. "We had a lot of fun. He's a genuinely nice guy." Who did genuinely nice things to her body—but sex did not a relationship make. And she had a future planned with Alan, even if none of it was official yet.

"Okay. Check in the *like* column. Was the sex good?"

"Hannah!"

"Right. Check in the *mind-blowing* column."

Shelby rolled her eyes but, since Hannah wasn't wrong, didn't argue.

"Do you want to see him again?"

"No." The answer came out firm—mostly because Shelby forced it out from between her lips that way.

Hannah leaned back. "Do we need to try that one again?"

Before Shelby could answer, Nolan's voice filled the room again, its low timbre seeming to rumble through all the sweet spots in her body. "Oh, yeah, baby. I should get shut out more often, because the phone lines are lighting up. Forget solar. We can power this town through my humiliation alone. Okay, caller one. What do you say? Should I just put my tail between my legs and walk away?"

"*Yes*," the very female voice said. "She's obviously a psycho-bitch not to want you."

Shelby's jaw dropped open.

"Just call me. I'll make it totally worth your while. Five-one-two, five—"

"Aaaannnnd thank you for that kind invitation, caller. We'll hear another opinion right after this musical look by the Chairmen of the Board into my broken psyche."

As his voice faded out, the classic *Gimme Just a Little More Time* filled the room.

"Not a bad idea," Hannah said. "Give the guy a chance."

"Hannah—"

"Look, I know you have a plan, and I know the idea of that" -she pointed toward the speakers with her eyes wide- "can be a little scary. I mean, the man's a bundle of slightly vulgar imagery, right?"

"He's a perfectly nice guy," Shelby said, then groaned when Hannah raised her brows. "I didn't mean—"

"Yes, you did. That's my point. He *is* a perfectly nice guy. Just because he's a little outside your box doesn't mean he's going to end up like your cousin or your uncle."

"Those are only the ones you know about," Shelby said. "Don't you get it? Nobody in my family until my parents even went to college. Real estate ownership is not a thing with them. And they wouldn't know a college fund if it bit them in the butt."

She drew in a breath. "They're all nice enough, I

guess. But we spent some time when I was growing up with my cousins, and we had nothing to talk about. All they did was watch television. And not even dramas or comedies. Nothing that we could actually talk about. No discussing themes or characters or even amusing commercials. They just watched shopping networks and ordered things then complained about having no money. Or they watched game shows and complained that they never won anything. And none of them seemed to care. They didn't want to get a better job or read a classic or, well, anything."

She sat back, exhausted from the passion of her words, and a little surprised that all of that had spilled out of her.

Hannah was leaning forward, her elbows on her thighs and her chin resting on her fists. "I totally get that," she said seriously. "My mom and I had a horrible time after my dad was killed, and her sister told her to just get on welfare. But she didn't. She scraped and clawed and ended up back in school. She worked as a teacher and learned how to pinch pennies so that she could put me through college."

"You do get it," Shelby said, relieved. She'd known that Hannah's policeman father was killed in the line of duty when she was a toddler, but she hadn't realized how hard her mother had scrambled.

"Yeah. And so do you. You know about college funds. And you understand mortgages. And you're ambitious. But what does this have to do with Nolan?"

Shelby stood, trying to put her thoughts into words. "See, this is why one-night stands are a bad idea. They never just go away after one night."

"That doesn't make them a bad idea," Hannah retorted. "It just means they're poorly named."

Despite herself, Shelby laughed. "It's just that Nolan doesn't fit, you know? I mean, he's all bawdy jokes and crazy pranks. But Alan's working for tenure and already thinking about a family."

"Hmm," Hannah said, and in the silence that followed, Shelby realized the song had ended and another one was coming to a close. Before Hannah continued, Nolan's voice filled the room again. "It's nine-fifty-eight, and that gives me just enough time to toss in a mention of my favorite bar, The Fix on Sixth. Trust me, peeps, you want to check this place out. Amazing food, fabulous drinks, and starting this Wednesday, a bi-weekly calendar contest for all you guys out there. And I don't mean for you to gawk at, I mean for you to get up on that stage, strut your stuff, and try to get yourself set up as Mr. January, because The Fix is filling up a calendar with a whole year full of men. Visit the website or drop by for details on how to enter."

"*Ohhhh,*" the female voice crooned. "*Twelve hunky men. I'll definitely have to ... come ... watch the contest.*"

"You do that, baby," Nolan said, as Shelby rolled her eyes and pointed at Hannah with an *I told you so* expression.

"We're at the top of the hour. And you know what that means—time for me to stop being Wayne. But if you haven't had your fill, tune in every weekday morning from six to ten for *Mornings with Wood*. I'm Nolan Wood, and you're listening to Sunny-side Saturdays."

"Enough of that," Hannah said, going to her phone and turning it off. "And before you say anything, it's his job. His schtick."

"I'm not so sure of that," Shelby said, smiling at the memory of some of Nolan's quips. But the truth was, if it wasn't for the fact that she wanted to win an argument, she wouldn't even be arguing the point. It was fun to talk to Nolan, no doubt about it. But that didn't mean he was the kind of guy she wanted to hitch her star to.

"I know what you're thinking," Hannah said.

"Bullshit."

"You're all the way down the road with this guy. Can't you just have fun with him? Why do you have to commit? Just *date*. Until Alan puts a ring on your finger, you need to explore what else is out there."

"I'll think about it," she said. "But it's probably a moot point. Despite his playlist, after yesterday, I doubt I'm ever going to see him again."

MANNY ORTEGA OWED NOLAN BIG-TIME.

First, instead of spending Saturday evening at The Fix with his buddies, he was in the ballroom at the Four Seasons hotel on the shores of Lady Bird Lake, the portion of the Colorado River that ran through downtown Austin. Second, he was wearing a damn tuxedo, and it was killing him to not tug at the collar. And third, Lauren and her politi-dweeb husband were on the premises.

Seriously, someone should just kill him now.

The only reason he was at the wedding of Brian Ross and Celia James was because Brian's father owned at least a dozen restaurants in the Austin area, not to mention three South Austin office complexes. His company was one of the most prolific advertisers on KIKX, and Manny considered Jonathon Ross to be just one step short of God. Which made his son Brian some sort of demi-god. Which apparently meant that Nolan—as a local celebrity—had to make an appearance and kiss his ass.

Not that Nolan really minded—he understood the way the business worked, and without sponsors, he was without work. And he was a big fan of the steady paycheck and the wonders that it could buy, food and shelter being tops of the list.

He just wished that the happy couple were people he'd met even once before. And he definitely wished that Lauren and Senator Studmuffin would acciden-tally fall in the river.

He'd skipped the actual nuptials, figuring that

neither bride nor groom nor their assorted relatives would notice his absence. And he'd offered his congratulations to the happy couple not long after the reception began, telling Brian how much he admired his father and complimenting the bride on her beautiful gown. She looked vaguely familiar, but since he was certain he'd never slept with her, he didn't waste too much time trying to place her.

Now, he was making the circuit—seeing and being seen until it was safe to cut and run.

When he saw the senator, he ducked around a partition that separated the main area from a makeshift cloakroom, and found himself face-to-face with Lauren.

Yup. An all around stellar evening.

"Nolan," she said, in a voice that dripped distaste. Honestly, how they'd shared a house for six months was one of the questions of the universe. "I didn't expect to see you here. Isn't there a monster truck rally tonight? Or a geek conference?"

"That was our problem, Lauren. You never even looked at me."

"The hell I didn't. The problem was that I *did* look, and I didn't respect what I saw. No ambition. I mean, minimum wage at some podunk radio station. We could have moved to LA."

"Not interested," he said. Once upon a time, he might have liked to be a big city DJ, but after he realized how much reading and paperwork the job actually entailed, the bloom on that dream faded. More than that, though, he loved Austin. He loved the people he worked with and the audience he'd built. He'd worked his ass off, and if Lauren couldn't see that—well, honestly, he didn't really give a fuck if she couldn't see that.

Except he did. Or, at least, he had.

Now, he realized, it wasn't Lauren's respect he wanted. It was another woman's. A woman who looked just as sexy in grandma-pumps and a shirt buttoned up to her collar as she did in fuck-me heels and a skin-tight dress. A woman he wished was by his side right then so he didn't have to suffer through this damn wedding by himself. No, he corrected, he wished that she *wanted* to be by his side. Too bad that wish wouldn't be coming true. After all, she'd made it pretty damn clear that despite the chemistry between them, she was putting the kibosh on any more explosions.

And, hell, he should be fine with that. Wasn't Lauren the reason he didn't date, unless you counted fucking, which he didn't. Dating was a relationship—a train in forward motion. A process of learning the subtle ins and outs of a woman and seeing if you fit together.

He wanted to walk that path with Shelby, and the fact that he couldn't seem to rip that desire out of his head preyed on him, especially since she was so very clearly uninterested.

"You know what?" Lauren said, her sharp voice jarring him from more pleasant thoughts, "I stand corrected. You *do* have ambition. But the things you aspire to simply don't interest me. Call me crazy, but it's never been my dream to come up with the perfect fart joke. Or to make fun of my own sex life. Then again," she added with a tight smile, "I guess yours probably *is* something to laugh about. At least, that's the way I remember it."

"Dammit, Lauren——"

"Down, boy," she said. "We're just talking. That's all you were doing on your radio show the other day, right? Teeth marks? Chilly vibes?" She leaned forward. "And you're right, Nolan, sweetie. Because I'm married to a senator now. I can bite your head off if I want. And all you'll be able to do about it is fire off a lame joke about your limp dick."

She patted him on the cheek, her painted lips pulled into a tight smile, then turned her back and walked away, wiggling her very toned ass in her very high heels.

"*Bitch.*" He didn't mean to speak aloud, but he couldn't hold it in, and a woman coming around the partition with a ticket to claim her checked purse frowned at him with distaste.

"Sorry," he muttered, feeling lower than a gutter. He went the opposite direction, sidling around the partition and ending up in some sort of darkened staging area that the hotel staff seemed to be using for dirty dishes. He drew a breath, gathering himself before he went out to say his final goodbyes, then realized he wasn't alone.

"I'm sorry," Shelby said. She reached for him, appeared to think better of it, and dropped her hand. "I didn't mean to eavesdrop."

"No problem," he said, the words coming out harsher than he'd intended. "Why wouldn't you be here to put a fucking cherry on my fucking perfect day?" He drew a breath, then shook his head, irritated with himself. "Sorry to have invaded your hideaway. I'll get going."

"Wait." This time when she reached for him, she held on, her hand warm and soft and very strong. He lifted his head prepared to tell her that he'd had a shit day and wasn't in the mood for games, but if she thought he'd ruined her perfect little life, too, then he'd be happy to introduce her to Lauren and they could swear some sort of blood oath and promise each other lifelong fealty.

But he never said the words, because she took a step closer, looked him right in the eyes, and said, "She's a bitch. And she's wrong. And—"

He had no idea what came next, because that's when he pulled her close, then shut her up with a long, slow kiss.

Chapter Ten

HIS KISS DESTROYED HER.

Shelby's head spun, her legs went weak, and the only thought she had in her head was that she wanted more. She hadn't planned this—hell, she'd only wanted to tell him that his ex was an idiot—but the instant that Nolan's lips touched hers, she was lost.

Maybe she should have realized. After all, she'd been craving him for days. He'd stolen into her dreams and barged into her thoughts. She'd spent hours justifying her decision to stay away when the only thing her body wanted was him since the moment he'd walked away Thursday morning.

Some small voice inside her head told her this was insane. That she should walk away now before she regretted it. That with this man she'd be risking more than her heart, she'd be risking her dreams —her plans.

She told the damn voice to shut up. She didn't care about protests or plans or the future. All she knew was now. And all she wanted was him.

What was it Hannah had said? That she should take a chance? Well, maybe Hannah hadn't convinced her, but Nolan's kisses were very, very persuasive.

"Nolan. Oh, God," she moaned as his mouth moved to her neck, her earlobe. He was working his magic on her, and heat flowed in her veins, a wild burning passion that his kisses only stoked, making her burn hotter and hotter until she was certain that she would simply combust in his arms.

She turned her head, forcing their mouths together again, and her fingers twined in his hair as she held him, tasted him. Christ, she craved him, and she opened her mouth to his, demanding he deepen the kiss, wanting to consume and be consumed.

She lost herself in the taste of him, in the taint of pain as his teeth tugged on her lower lip. In the coppery tang of blood from the violent clashing of their mouths and teeth. It wasn't enough—it wasn't nearly enough. And even when he pulled away, his mouth closing over the halter of her dress so that he sucked her nipple through the material, and his hands started to slide under her skirt, she simply wanted *more*. So badly—so desperately—that when he pulled away and stood in front of her, she actually whimpered.

"Don't stop. God, Nolan, please don't stop."

"Hell no," he said. "But we need to take a short recess to find a better place fast. Otherwise, I'm taking you in the ladies' room and locking us into a stall."

"No good," she teased. "No way I could stay quiet enough."

He chuckled. "Good. I like your noises. I like to make you scream."

"Make me come and I'll scream as loud as you want," she murmured, and Nolan tilted his head back and laughed.

"What?"

"Listen to you. How many people know what naughty things can come out of that mouth? You with your sensible shoes and your tweed jacket and your tailored button down shirts."

She lifted her brows. "From anyone else, I'd think I'd been insulted."

"Oh, no," he said. "Not even close. You're my fantasy, baby. Did you know that? Because you're all mine." His eyes searched hers as his fingertip stroked her cheek. "No one else sees the woman I do."

She swallowed. "Nolan…"

"You gave that to me, Shelby, whether you meant to or not."

His words were like a soft rain, and she soaked them in, knowing he was right. He saw a part of her no one else did. Certainly not Alan, who'd probably die from shock if he had even an inkling of the things she'd done and said with Nolan.

"Do you have any idea how much of a turn on that is?" Nolan asked. "Knowing we have this secret? That you've shared something so intimate with me?"

"I do," she whispered. "Because if I'm your fantasy, then you're my muse." She brushed a kiss over his lips. "I've never done these things with anyone," she told him. "You inspire me."

"Do I? What are you inspired to do now?"

"Nothing we can do right here," she said, then laughed.

"Where, then?"

"I know." She took his hand. "Come on."

She and the other girls from Brandywine had rented a room at the hotel for the night. No one intended to actually stay in it, but that way they had a private place to rest, leave make-up, change clothes if they needed to, and simply get away from the crowd if it all became too overwhelming.

"I had four cousins get married over six months," Kayla had said when she'd suggested the room. "Trust me when I say it's totally worth the expense."

Right about now, Shelby was enthusiastically agreeing with Kayla's assessment. All the other girls were still in the ballroom dancing and gossiping and drinking champagne. Which meant that the room was entirely free—and Shelby intended to take full advantage.

"You have a room?" Nolan asked as she led him to the door at the end of an eighth floor hall.

"I believe in being prepared," she said, then added, "Call it the girl-power staging area," as she led him into the clothing strewn, make-up scattered housekeeping horror that came from five girls sharing a room. Even if it was only to change and freshen up.

He glanced around. "Are we alone?"

"Completely," she said, finishing the word on a gasp because he had her back up against the wall, her arms above her head, her crossed wrists held tight in his hand. She was helpless, and he moved in fast, taking her mouth with his, claiming her, controlling her.

His lips possessed her. Owned her. And his free hand led an exploratory charge, pulling her breasts free from the halter-style bodice. "You look good enough to eat," he teased before lowering his mouth to her breast.

He scraped his teeth along her nipple, causing a wild sensation to build in her sex. She moaned, squeezing her legs together and shifting her hips, hoping to increase the friction.

"Someone likes."

"Someone does," she confirmed, then gasped at the sound of footsteps stopping right outside the door.

"Fuck," she whispered as she shifted out from under him, took his hand, and sprinted for the bathroom.

They burst in and locked the bathroom door before her anonymous roomie burst through the main door. A moment of muffled noise, then the bathroom door knob rattled. Shelby glanced at Nolan, who actually looked amused, the bastard.

"I'm in here," she said, sitting on the edge of the tub because her legs were shaky. "I'm a little sick."

"Oh no," Leslie said. "Let me in and we'll help you out."

"Oh, God, no," she said, but not in response to Leslie's comment, but to the fact that Nolan had dropped to the ground, spread her knees, and buried his face between her legs.

"What?" Leslie called.

"I just mean I'd rather be alone. Too much alcohol is all." Her voice sounded rough, and she supposed that made it more convincing. But as he sucked on her clit through her thin cotton panties, she decided she really didn't care.

Shifting, she spread her legs wider and held on to the edge of the tub for dear life as he tugged the crotch of her panties aside and worked magic with his tongue.

"I was going to freshen my make-up," Les called, "but I'll just use what's in my purse."

"Uh-huh," Shel said as Nolan sucked on her clit while teasing her labia with a finger wet with her desire.

"Are you coming later?" Les asked.

"Oh, God, yes, absolutely," Shelby cried out, as Nolan's magical tongue took her loudly and fabulously over the edge.

Nolan, she mouthed when she came back to earth, but he just pulled her down to the area rug, then yanked her panties around her knees as her sex pulsed in anticipation.

"Condom" he whispered, and she spread her hands helplessly.

"Five girls. Someone must have one," he said. Then he was on his feet searching. A moment later he thrust a silver package into the air.

"Hurry," she said, not bothering to be quiet anymore. She thought she'd heard Les leave. And if she was wrong, well, she didn't care.

He opened the fly of his tux pants, then knelt between her legs as she reached for him, wanting to touch his cock before he sheathed it. "Don't," he said. "I'm too close. And you don't want to stain that dress."

She burst out laughing, and he got on top of her, laughing, too. Then he was inside her and their sounds were laughter and pleasure and wild, glorious fun.

And when he came, she hooked her legs around him and used her strength to pull him in deeper, closer to her core. Closer to her heart.

When he was spent, he stretched out beside her, his finger tracing her collar bone. "You're incredible," he said. "And I bet we just had the most fun of anybody at this wedding.

Chapter Eleven

"THINKING ABOUT JUMPING IN?" Nolan asked, coming to stand at the end of the dock beside Amanda.

She turned her head and smiled at him. "I haven't swum in Lake Austin since we were kids." She sat down, hanging her bare feet over the edge. "And most of the time you threw me in, you jerk. I rarely had the chance to jump."

He dropped down beside her, his own flip-flops now abandoned on the wooden dock. "That's what big brothers are for."

She looked at him sideways. "Is *that* what they're for? I never could figure that out."

"Cute."

She nudged his shoulder. "What are Mom and Dad up to?"

Technically, they were his Mom and her Dad, but their parents had married when they were both so young that neither he nor Amanda thought of themselves as stepsiblings. Except when the topic of his asshole father came up. Then Nolan felt about as far removed from the Franklin family as was humanly possible.

"When I walked down," he told her, "Dad was watching a documentary on bees, and Mom was cleaning up after lunch."

"Dammit," Amanda said, "I told her I'd do that when I got back."

"Yeah, right. Like that would happen."

She grinned. "That was my trick as a kid. But as a responsible adult, I really did intend to clean up. Only seemed fair since she put out the Sunday spread. Exactly what about bees?"

"No idea. But Mom doesn't mind. Says it keeps him out of trouble."

A retired petroleum engineer, for the last five years, Huey Franklin had become inexplicably addicted to nature documentaries.

"Speaking of trouble," Amanda began with a wicked little grin, "I guess you got it all worked out?"

"Color me confused."

"The girl," she said. "Trying to get some girl. Not getting the girl. Much musical and comedic angst on the radio. And then no angst, so I'm assuming you and the girl worked it out. Oh, and the spot you did for The Fix was great. Jenna said they really appreciate it." She paused, then laughed. "Don't look at me like that. What? You thought I didn't listen to your show?"

"I didn't think about it at all, actually." He pulled an exaggerated frown. "And you can tell Jenna I've got more in mind. Maybe interview some of the calendar guys. Tyree, too, if he's willing. And I thought about live streaming some of the contest if they're cool with that."

"Love the idea."

"As for you listening to my show, I'm not sure if I'm flattered that you're interested or mortified that my sister hears all my X-rated bullshit."

"Oh, please. Like you ever censor yourself around me. And I think it's more PG-13. Maybe NC-17. But only when you manage to slip something past Connor."

He laughed. "You make a good point."

"I always do," she countered. "And you're changing the subject."

Amanda always was too clever by half. But considering all the help she gave him over the years, he'd never razzed her on her brainiac ways. "You're right. The girl has been gotten."

"Nice. So who is she? And don't just say she's a girl. I got that part already."

"She's definitely *not* just a girl."

"Oh, really?" She ran her toes through the water and flicked her foot up, sprinkling both of them with droplets. "I want a name."

"But you're not getting one. We're not public yet." They'd talked about it briefly while they were on the floor of the bathroom in the Four Seasons. The fact that they both wanted more of each other. And the fact that there were complications.

"Really? Why not?"

"Partly because I want to hold it close. Partly because there's this guy she was seeing who doesn't know yet, and partly because she doesn't want to be known as the girl I talked about on the radio."

"Go public now, and it's obvious she's the same girl," Amanda said, nodding with understanding.

"Exactly."

"Well, have fun with your covert sexcapades, and introduce me when you can."

"You got it. By the way, you're coming to the benefit, right? It's only a few weeks away."

"You know I am, idiot. For one thing, I'm on the committee. For another, my firm is buying a table. For a third, do you really think I'd miss it?"

He didn't. Not really. The benefit was for the Dyslexia Reading & Tutoring Room, and he was this year's keynote speaker. Considering he spoke for a living, he was remarkably nervous.

"I had to make sure," he told her. "Are Mom and Dad at your table?"

"Yup. Is your dad coming?"

He gaped at her, and after a moment, she cringed.

"Sorry. I should know better. I guess I thought—hoped—that maybe he'd.... Well, anyway, he's a rat bastard."

"Not arguing."

She took his hand. "But Nolan, it doesn't matter. When you're up on that podium, you need to remember just how much *he* doesn't matter."

He nodded, pushing down the memories of the dark days he'd been forced to spend with his birth father. Goddamn joint custody. The man was an ass. Not that he abused Nolan, but his sharp tongue sure could shame.

He reached for Amanda's hand and gave it a squeeze, remembering how much she'd been at his side during those years. Hell, she'd been his goddamn lifeline. "You'll be front and center, right?"

"You better believe it, big brother."

———————

BETWEEN HER DEADLINES and Nolan's crazy schedule of on-air performances and public appearances, it was days before they had the chance to go out again. But with her **KIKX** live-streaming app, at least she had Nolan in the morning—and so did all the other women in town.

The thought gave Shelby a little thrill. She'd have to be blind not to know how many women were interested in the man—or, for that matter, how many he'd slept with in the past. But he was with her now, and she believed him when he'd told her that there was no other woman in his life, with the non-relevant exception of his sister and mother, of course.

His radio banter certainly seemed to prove that point. Bawdy and funny as usual, there were no references to Nolan's own sex life, short of a couple of riffs on the title of the show and him waking up frustrated and alone the last few mornings.

She fully intended to give him grief about that—and offer to let him crash at her place if he wanted to take care of any mornings with wood before *Mornings With Wood*.

Any references to her—or to them—were thankfully completely absent from the airwaves.

At least, she told herself she was thankful.

The trouble was, she didn't entirely believe her rational, sane conclusion that she was pleased not to be the subject of his jokes. And the realization that maybe—just maybe—there'd been something a little titillating about being the impetus behind a wild blast of a song like George Michaels' *I Want Your Sex* was more than a little disconcerting.

Not that she had time to ponder any hidden ambition to be comedy fodder. On the contrary, Frank was keeping her crazy busy. And when the receptionist buzzed just before lunch on Wednesday to tell her that the lunch she ordered had arrived and could she send the delivery guy back, Shelby had almost bit the poor woman's head off with her reply that *of course* she could. The point of delivery was that Shelby didn't want to leave her desk—not even to schlep down to reception.

Only after she'd ended the call did she realize that she hadn't ordered any take-out. *Great.* Now she was going to have to waste time figuring out whose lunch she was about to get.

"Come in," she called in response to the tap at her door. "Listen, there's been a mix-*oh!*"

It was Nolan.

He was standing right on her threshold, looking ridiculously sexy in faded jeans that hugged his thighs and a black KIKX tee. He also wore a Longhorns baseball cap and carried a paper bag from Wholy Bagels, which he extended toward her as he stepped all the way into her office, closing the door behind him.

"No way," she said, taking the bag and clutching it to her heart. "You brought me a bagel? I love this place."

"I know," he said, then added, "You had a bag of bagels on your counter and some of their spreads in your fridge the first time I was at your house. I took a chance that you liked them for lunch, too."

That had been the first time they'd made love. A night that had been frantic and wild and utterly awesome. She'd been doing good the next morning to notice if she was wearing clothes before she left the house. The fact that he noticed a detail like bagels blew her away.

"I love bagels for lunch," she confirmed. "I don't even toast them. Just slather on the cream cheese. But you went all the way to South Austin to get me lunch?"

He came closer, took the bag and dropped it on her desk, then pulled her close. "I'd go further than that," he said, then kissed her lightly. "Although too far and it might defeat the purpose."

She frowned, and he laughed. "If I went to Dallas for your lunch, I wouldn't be back until after dinner."

She rolled her eyes. "Goof."

"That's why they pay me the not-so-big-but-market-appropriate bucks."

Sighing, she hugged him tight. "Thanks," she said. "I wish I could invite you into a conference room to eat with me, but I have to get this revised spreadsheet to Frank before one, and—"

"And I only came for delivery," he said, extricating himself from her embrace. "Although, if this was a porn film, I'd climb under your desk and distract you while you worked. A little cream cheese in some interesting places…"

"Interesting's one word for it," she said.

"Delicious is another."

"Perv."

"Only for you."

"Now you're a liar, too," she teased.

"Not even a little bit."

A warm glow spread over her skin, and she sighed happily. "Actually, if this was a porn movie, I'd give you a tip." She eased in closer, then cupped her hand over his cock. "Too bad I don't do porn."

He put his hand over hers, and she felt him stiffen even more beneath the denim. "Too bad indeed."

Her pulse picked up tempo and she tilted her head back to meet his eyes. "You're like some magical talisman, you know that, right? Because this really isn't me."

He kissed her softly on the tip of her nose. "Maybe it is."

The words rocked through her, both obvious and yet disturbing. At the same time, he stepped back, extricating himself with two words, "Rain check."

"You're on."

"How does tonight sound? It's the first Man of the Month contest at The Fix tonight. Want to come with me?"

She did. Desperately. But she wasn't sure she was ready to be public just yet. At the very least, there were things she needed to clear. "I—I can't," she said. "I already have plans."

"Oh."

It was perverse, but the disappointment in his voice was profoundly flattering.

"We're still on for Friday, though," she said. "Aren't we?"

His smile bloomed. "Hell, yes, we are."

Chapter Twelve

"YOU'RE FIDGETY," Alan said, passing her the bread-basket that the waiter just delivered. "Is anything wrong?"

She shook her head as she looked around the well-appointed interior of The Roaring Fork, an upscale restaurant in the Stephen F. Austin Intercontinental Hotel. "When you called this morning to suggest dinner, I was expecting a burger. Maybe Tex-Mex. I'm a mess." Her suit was fine, but she'd gone to the gym at five, and then had hurried to meet Alan at the Starbucks on Sixth and Congress without fixing her make-up and with her hair pulled back into a messy ponytail.

"You look beautiful," he said. "And I thought we should celebrate."

"Oh? What are we celebrating?" Her eyes widened. "Did the dean talk to you about tenure?"

He laughed. "Not yet. No, it's been four months since your mother introduced us."

"Oh." She sat back. "Has it really?" Strange that it didn't seem that long. They were close in so many ways, and yet there was a formality between them that felt a little bit like they were living in a Jane Austen novel. She'd known Nolan much less time, and yet with him she felt like—well, like herself.

A waiter arrived with a dozen oysters on the half-shell and a bottle of champagne. She watched him pop the cork, then pour, and all the while prickly fingers of dread crept up the back of her neck.

"Alan…" She trailed off, not sure what to say. Hell, not sure what *he* intended to say.

"I wanted this to be special," he said, reaching into his jacket pocket.

"Alan, wait. We—"

He held up a hand to silence her. "Please. This isn't what you think."

Her shoulders sagged with relief, but then tensed again when he put a ring box in front of her. She looked up, meeting his eyes, completely confused.

"It's not an engagement ring. I know you—*we're*—not ready for that."

Oh, God.

"But please, open it."

She couldn't force her hands to move. "Shouldn't we talk—"

He picked up the box, then flipped the lid open,

revealing a simple silver band with small diamonds around an ornate heart. "It's a promise ring," he said, looking so pleased with himself it broke her heart. "I texted a picture to your mother. She said she was certain the style would suit you."

"It's very pretty," she agreed, "but—"

"I want this to represent our promise to each other to move forward with this relationship. We've never talked about being exclusive before, but I want that, Shelby. I want only you."

He took the ring out of the box and held it out to her. Time slowed, and when she saw his forehead crease, she realized she was slowly shaking her head and holding her hands tight in her lap.

"Shelby?"

"Alan." She had to take a sip of water and swallow in order to continue. "Alan, I'm so sorry. I—I can't accept this."

He blinked, then sat back, the ring still in his hand. "I see. Is it too soon?"

"Yes, I mean, no." She sucked in a breath. "I mean I've met someone else and … oh, God, Alan, I wanted to talk to you about this tonight. I never dreamed it would be like this, though."

"So you don't want to be exclusive," he said. "That's fair. It's only been a few months, and I'd never want you to commit without being certain, and if process of elimination—"

"Alan, no." She reached out and closed her hand

over his. "You're a great guy—you really are. And before I thought—" She cut herself off with a shake of her head. "It doesn't matter. The point is, I don't know if this guy will end up being the one for me. But I do know that seeing him has made me think more about myself and what I want. And what I don't want."

"Me," he said.

"I'm sorry." Her instinct was to say more. To ramble and try to smooth. To try to make it all better. But that wasn't in her power, especially not since she was the one doing the hurting. And so she simply shut up and let him deal with the reality she'd thrust upon him.

He took a sip of water, then rearranged the salt and pepper shakers. "I'm sorry, too," he finally said. "But maybe it's good I made this misstep. Who knows how long we would have gone on pretending?"

She winced a little, because he was right. She'd intended to tell him tonight—but in all honesty, they should have had this talk days ago.

"Do you still want dinner?"

She hesitated, her glass of water almost to her lips. "Seriously?"

A small smile touched the corner of his mouth. "Be kind of hypocritical if I stopped liking you now, wouldn't it?"

She laughed, then shook her head. "You really are

a good man, Alan Lowe. And someday, some woman is going to be very lucky to have you."

———

NOLAN LEFT The Fix with a spring in his step. The first Man of the Month contest had been a huge success, and not just because Jenna and her team had managed to cajole a dozen local guys into entering. And not because there'd been a line down the block to get in.

Not even because the women in the audience went absolutely apeshit when the guys strutted their stuff across the stage.

No, as far as Nolan was concerned, Reece Walker had made the whole fucking evening because he'd stood on that stage and confessed his love to Jenna Montgomery.

Nolan had listened to the words, but his eyes had been on Jenna, and the expression on her face had mesmerized him. The soft sweet glow of joy that had seemed to light up the entire bar.

He wanted a woman to look at him like that.

No. Not *a* woman. He wanted Shelby.

She'd snuck up on him, that was for damn sure, but there was no question in his mind or his heart that he wanted her. And, please God, he was pretty damn sure that she wanted him, too, and for more than a casual fuck, no matter how fabulous those fucks might be.

He was walking west on Sixth Street, and he paused at Congress and waited for the light to change. He needed to turn left to get to his condo, but something caddy corner to him, right in front of the Starbucks, caught his eye.

Shelby.

And she was with a man in sport coat and close-cropped hair. Someone from her office, maybe?

He started to call to her, but then she lifted up onto her toes, put her hand on his shoulder, and kissed him.

What the fuck?

What the bloody, goddamn fuck?

She waved, then continued down the street, presumably returning to the Frost Building, to get her car and go home.

He told himself he should drop it. He had a show to do in the morning. But it wasn't that late and he knew damn well that he wouldn't sleep until he saw her. So, screw it. He was going to be *that guy.*

He pulled out his phone, tapped his favorite ride share app, and snagged a car. Since she lived barely over a mile away, he was at her house and on her front porch even before she got home. Assuming she was coming home.

Maybe she was going to his house. Whoever *he* was.

He threaded his fingers together behind his neck and tilted his head back to look at the stars. He had it bad. He hadn't seen it coming, but damned if he didn't have it bad.

This woman had the power to break his heart—and that scared him to death.

He was pacing—rehearsing—ten minutes later when her car pulled into the drive. She killed the engine, got out, and walked toward her door with her head down as she rummaged in her purse for her keys.

He gaped at her, wishing that keyless cars had never been invented, because then she'd have her keys in her hand right now. Because what if he was an attacker? Did she have absolutely no sense of personal security? He was going to have to have a long talk with her. Maybe have Brent install some motion sensitive lights and a push button lock on her front door. He wanted her safe, after all, and—

"Nolan?" She smiled at him, wide and bright, as if she hadn't completely knocked his world off kilter not fifteen minutes ago by making out with some asswipe. "What are you doing here?"

"You fucking kissed him," he blurted. Which *really* wasn't what he rehearsed, and he knew damn well that it wasn't the best approach under the circumstances.

As if the universe wanted to prove him right, he

saw her posture shift as her spine straightened and her chin lifted. "You were *spying* on me?"

"I was walking down Congress. And imagine my surprise when I find you sucking face with some dude. I mean, Christ, Shelby, we're dating."

She crossed her arms over her chest and glared at him. "Is that what we're doing?"

"Well, we're damn sure seeing a lot of each other, especially when you factor in how often we're naked. And *whoopsie*, but my penis just seems to keep landing in your vagina. So I figure we're either dating or one of us is pretty damn clumsy."

She twisted, looking back and forth at the neighboring houses. "What is wrong with you?"

"Guess I'm just the class clown. You planning on dumping me for the valedictorian?"

For a moment, she looked like she was about to really let him have it. But all she did was stand perfectly still, probably counting to ten. Finally, she jammed her key into the door, then held it open and gestured roughly. "In," she ordered. "We are *not* doing this in front of the neighbors."

Doing this. The words sat like lead in his stomach. Doing what? Breaking up? *Shit, fuck, cocksucker, mother-fucker, cunt, tits, piss.*

He drew in a breath, nodded calmly, and walked over the threshold.

She followed, then slammed the door behind her. "Let's get a few things straight," she said, coming over and poking him in the chest with her index finger. "First, I am not your ice princess bitch of an ex-wife. Got it?"

She didn't give him a chance to answer. Just barreled on. "Second, that *dude* was Alan." The name struck him like a kick in the gut.

"*Fuck*." He almost choked on the word. "So, what does that mean?" Did she want to break up? Because no matter what she said, they were damn sure dating. To hell with that. He wasn't going without a fight.

Or, rather, a bigger fight than this one.

"Third," she continued, completely ignoring his question. "You're an idiot."

"Because I fell for you? Yeah, maybe I am."

"You're an idiot because it was a good-bye kiss. A very chaste good-bye kiss that seemed appropriate since I'd just broken up with him."

"You—" He tried to continue the sentence, but his thoughts were too muddled.

She crossed her arms over her chest, tilted her head, and waited.

"You broke up with him?"

"I figured I had to. I can hardly keep going out with him when I feel this way about you. But he's a sweet man who never did anything wrong except not be you. So don't you dare give me shit."

"Ah," he said, shoving his hand into the pockets of his jeans. "And how exactly do you feel about me?"

She flashed a crooked smile then stepped closer

until she could wrap her arms around him. "Like you're the kind of guy my vagina keeps sneaking up on."

He couldn't help it; he barked out a laugh.

"You're not too bright though, are you? I mean, falling for an idiot like me."

"No," she agreed. "Not very bright at all." She brushed a kiss over his lips. "You want to keep fighting or would you like some coffee?"

"Got any Scotch?"

She laughed. "Yeah, I think I can hook you up. Hang on."

As she went to the kitchen to get the drink, he settled in on the couch. And the first thing he noticed was that there was a new book on the coffee table —*Watchmen*

"You're reading this?" he asked when she brought him the drink.

"Barely started," she said. "I called and got the folks at *Dragon's Lair* to put aside a copy for me," she added, referring to his favorite store for gaming and graphic novels. "You said it was good," she added, as if daring him to contradict her.

"It is," he said, feeling ridiculously, stupidly flattered that she'd shelved some thick classic tome in favor of his favorite graphic novel.

"In that case, I have an idea for the rest of the evening. Wanna snuggle on the couch, read *Watchmen* together, and later on we can see if any of our body parts tumble into each other?"

"Yeah," he said, hooking one arm around her shoulder as he reached for the book. "I think that sounds like a stellar idea."

Chapter Thirteen

"SO YOU TWO ARE GETTING SERIOUS," Kayla said as she and Hannah and Shelby roamed the aisles of Toy Joy—Austin's go-to place for silly, wacky, and unusual toys for kids and adults. It was lunch hour on Tuesday and they were on a quest for the perfect gift for Kayla's eight-year-old niece.

"I guess we are," Shelby said, unable to hold back her grin. It had been almost a week since Nolan had lost his shit over her kissing Alan, and things between them had upticked during the intervening days. They spent most evenings together at either her house or his condo; they'd driven out to the Hill Country to shop and taste wine—an outing that her friends all considered a "relationship checkmark"—and though they never ran out of things to talk about, they could just as easily enjoy each other's silence without the pressure of having to fill the space with small talk.

None of that—with the exception of the Hill Country—would be on Kayla's radar. Which meant that she was judging the state of their relationship by the content of Nolan's radio show. And, he'd asked Shelby's permission before he said a single word.

"You're sure?" he'd double-checked when she'd told him it was fine. And when she'd assured him it was, he'd asked her to tell him why. Apparently he wasn't taking any chances on pissing her off again,

"Honestly, I'm not sure I can explain it. But listening to you—even back when I was mad at you that time—it was like seeing a different side of myself."

"What do you mean?"

"You make everything fun. Traffic. The weather. Sex."

"Sex *is* fun."

"True," she'd said. "But before you, I never thought of it that way. Nice, yes. Mind-blowing, sometimes. But fun? Like actually laughing while you're naked?" She shook her head. "A billion times no."

His brow furrowed. "Really?"

She just kissed him. "Don't get any ideas. No going off and starting a new career as a sex guru, okay? And if you're talking about me, then it damn well better be anonymous."

"Got it," he said, and from then on, anytime he referred to his "partner in crime and in bed," he called her his Paradox.

She'd asked him why, and he'd told her that was how he'd thought of her the very first night they met. Shy and quiet, but with an inferno inside. "And it's still the same," he'd added, unbuttoning her plain white blouse and then lifting her skirt to tug down her pantyhose.

"I should buy you a garter and thong, but I've come to like unwrapping the package," he'd said, then dropped to his knees and used his tongue to make her come so hard and so fast she thought she might die right then.

All in all, that had been a fabulous way to end the workday.

"You should call in to his show sometime," Hannah said. "That would be a hoot."

She shook her head. "You guys know it's me. And I'm sure some of his friends do, too. But what if my clients were listening? Or my mother?"

"So? It's not like he's talking about robbing banks," Kayla said. "You're dating. It's all good."

"Good, yes. Public, no." In theory, she had to admit it would be fun to call in to tease him. Or to suggest all sorts of decadent things they could do together. But of course she'd never do it. No way was she risking the world knowing that she was the woman on the other side of those racy, bawdy stories he told.

And her dirty little secret? She kind of liked it. Being anonymous. Being a mystery woman. And then hearing about their lives through the unique filter of a man who'd come to mean so much to her.

"I bought you something," Hannah said, her eyes twinkling as they left Toy Joy with all sorts of silly gizmos and gadgets for themselves, along with an awesome pretend veterinarian kit.

"Yeah?" Shelby said as Hannah passed her a small wrapped box about five inches cubed. "What is it?"

"Open it tonight. Use it in the morning."

"Hannah!"

"I'm serious. You'll thank me."

Shelby looked dubiously at the small gift. "If you say so."

She did as Hannah had told her, and waited until the evening to open it—then laughed like a loon when she saw it.

Yeah, this was good.

Not only was the present brilliant, but she was glad to have it on this night, because she'd needed the laugh. She hadn't spent a night without Nolan in about a week, and she was feeling a little lonely and out of sorts. But he was doing some sort of broadcaster's event downtown that would run late, and since he had to be up before dawn, he'd told her he would just crash at his condo and then see her Wednesday evening when they went to The Fix together to watch The Man of the Month contest and tape a few snippets for Nolan to promote on his show.

The night was rough, and when the alarm startled

her awake at six, she realized how quickly she'd grown accustomed to sleeping with Nolan's warmth beside her.

She scrubbed her hands over her face, then reached for Hannah's present—an electronic voice changer that could be used to talk anonymously on a phone. It undoubtedly wouldn't fool the CIA, but under the circumstances, it was absolutely perfect.

Armed with her toy, she sat up in bed, dialed the KIKX request line, crossing her fingers that Nolan would answer and not Connor, his producer. Thankfully, fate was on her side. "Hey, caller. Welcome to *Mornings With Wood*. What's your request?"

"More of you, for a start," she said in her weirdly electronic voice. "I missed you last night."

There was a pause—and since Nolan *never* left dead air, she knew she'd flummoxed him and did a little mental happy dance. The pause was barely noticeable, though. And since no one ad-libbed better than Nolan, he was soon with the program.

"I think I'm the one that missed you," he said. "And to you listeners out there, this is one hell of a rare treat. Because you are listening to a real live paradox. And now the question is—did she call to chat, to make a request, or for something wicked and naughty? Personally, I'm hoping for option three. But I'm not holding my breath. I know her, remember, and she's really not a morning person."

Despite herself, Shelby laughed. "A request," she

said, her heart pounding foolishly from nerves. "For a song … and for later."

"Let's have it."

"The Veronicas. *Take Me On The Floor.*"

She heard the raw sound he made through the phone, and then heard it continue into a growl when she turned the volume up on the radio. She'd hung up abruptly, and even though that was lame, she could already feel her underarms sweating and her heart pounding and all she did was call in to the show.

How on earth did Nolan do that every day? And unscripted? It was a freaking feat of genius as far as she was concerned.

She turned up the volume on her radio, then listened as Nolan riffed about her call, then upped the ante by playing a snippet from the Starlight Vocal Band's *Afternoon Delight.*

And as that song faded out and her requested song faded in, he spoke firmly and clearly during the transition. "Be home at noon, Paradox," he ordered. "And be naked."

SHELBY BROKE every traffic law on the books racing to get home for lunch. She had to; she was running ridiculously late.

Frank had pulled her aside in the elevator bank to let her know that the firm had bought a table at an upcoming benefit for some charity, and that he wanted her to go so that she could mingle with prospective clients.

But the benefit was more than two weeks away, and she *really* didn't need to be talking about it now. Not when floor sex was waiting for her at home—and she desperately had to run an errand before hand.

She'd finally taken the brochure he shoved into her hands, promised she'd read it carefully, then crammed it into her briefcase once she was alone on the elevator.

Honestly. Did the man have no respect for the sanctity of the long lunch?

Thankfully, she made it to her place with five minutes to spare, and she raced inside, stripped off her clothes, then flopped naked onto her couch just as she heard the key she'd given Nolan jiggle in the lock.

"Oh, no, baby," he said, his eyes raking over her as he entered. "That's a lovely picture, but the game was on the floor, remember?"

"So take me there," she teased, making him laugh and come to her side.

"You think I'm going to toss you over my shoulder and then lay you out on the floor? No way, baby. Way too predictable."

He turned around, then pushed the coffee table all the way into the center of the room, making her wonder what deliciously seductive activity he had planned. But when he crept up on her and started tickling her, she laughed and screamed and kicked until she fell onto the floor cursing his name and his family and all his descendants until the end of time.

His end game became clear when he had her pinned down, his body straddling hers, his hands holding hers above her head. She was breathing hard, they both were, and there was a vulnerability to being naked while he was clothed that turned her on.

She bit her lower lip, and met his eyes. "Do it," she said. "Take me right here on the floor."

He almost laughed, but the humor died soon as he slid down her body, spreading her wide before he hustled out of his jeans, then kissed his way up her body, forcing her legs to stay wide apart despite the way she squirmed, searching for maximum friction.

And when he'd kissed and teased ever inch of her body—when she was wet and limp and needy—that's when he positioned himself over her, his cock at her core. "Are you ready?"

"For you? Always."

He took her then. Wild and deep, with his eyes locked on hers the entire time, never looking away even when they both came together in an orgasm that shook the house, and fused him tightly to her heart.

Chapter Fourteen

SHELBY SQUARED the corners of the books stacked on her coffee table, then fluffed the cushions on the couch. She liked the house tidy, and she'd gotten into the habit of spending a few hours every Saturday making sure the place was in shape.

What she hadn't done lately was clean out her briefcase, and even though that was a job that made more sense to tackle at work, she'd already conquered the kitchen, the bathroom and the living room, and she was still in the mood to kick some organizational butt.

Since her house was too tiny for a full-size dining table to spread out on, she moved to the bedroom and dumped the contents of her cherished Louis Vuitton briefcase onto the fluffy white spread. The case had been a present to herself after she passed her CPA exam, and she loved it because it held so much stuff, traveled everywhere with her, and still looked great.

She was sorting all the papers into piles when she heard footsteps on her front porch and then the sound of a key in the lock. She was just about to abandon her project and go meet Nolan in the living room when she caught sight of the benefit brochure that Frank had pressed on her days ago.

The cover said only DTRR with a stylized graphic of letters and words in odd shapes and sizes. Since that gave her no clue as to what cause the sponsoring organization supported, she started to flip the pages, wanting at least a little information to throw at Nolan before she asked if he wanted to join her.

"Hey," he said, coming into the bedroom and leaning on the dresser about the time that she realized that DTRR was the Dyslexia Training and Resource Room, an organization devoted to helping children with dyslexia.

"Hey, back." She glanced up at him, greeting his smile with one of her own before looking back down, more interested in the benefit now that she knew it was for a good cause. "I was just trying to figure out what this benefit Frank has me going to is about. I think I may need a date," she teased, and was surprised to see that the bright humor in his face had faded.

"Something the mat—"

She didn't finish the question, because while she

was speaking, she glanced down at the brochure. And there—on the center spread—was one of Nolan's publicity shots and the large font announcement that the longtime DTRR supporter would be this year's keynote speaker at the gala dinner, talking for the first time publicly about his lifetime struggle with dyslexia.

With a frown, she looked back up at him. "You're the keynote speaker? The guest of honor?"

He nodded, and she pushed off the bed, then started to pace. "You didn't tell me."

"Tell you what?"

She whipped around to face him. He had his arms crossed over his chest, his posture defensive, and for some reason, that irritated her all the more.

"Don't play games, Nolan. You didn't tell me you were headlining a gala benefit. You didn't invite me to be your date even though we've been sleeping together for quite a while now."

"Is that what we're doing? Sleeping together?"

She ignored him. "And you somehow failed to mention that you're dyslexic."

His jaw tightened. "It didn't exactly come up in the conversation."

Cold anger bubbled inside her. But anger she could handle. It was the hurt that was making her legs shaky and tears gather in her throat. "You kept a huge part of yourself from me. You didn't let me in at all."

Some of the tension left his body, and his expression turned soft and earnest. "It was private. Intensely personal. And not something that's easy to talk about. I debated for months before I agreed to speak at the benefit."

"Intensely personal," she repeated. "Do you have any idea how hard it was for me to wrap my head around the idea that you turned our sex life into fodder for your show? Or to ask you to tie my wrists when you made love to me? That's not me—doing it or asking it. But I managed it—hell, I wanted it—because it was you. Because I thought that we were a couple."

A tear trickled down the side of her nose, and she brusquely wiped it away.

"Baby, we are…"

"Are we? Because it doesn't feel that way right now. It feels like all I've seen is the celebrity. Have you ever shown me the man?"

"Okay, wait a second," he said. "That's harsh."

"Is it? You make your whole life public for ratings, but I always thought you held some of it back. That there was a part of you—an intimate part—that you let the people close to you see. And maybe it was my fault for thinking I fell into that group. But I don't, Nolan. As far as you're concerned, I'm just another woman in your audience getting the watered-down, sexed-up version of you."

"That's not fair."

She blinked, her body tired, her head hurting. "Isn't it? It feels fair. Hell, it feels like the truth.

Because, dammit, Nolan, it hurts. Here," she said with her hand over her heart. "And I'm not sure how to make it feel better."

———

SHE CURLED up on the bed after he left, and she was still there hours later when her mom called around dinnertime. "I spoke with Alan," she said without preamble. "Is it true that you broke up with him?"

Shelby rubbed her face and forced herself to sit up. She needed blood to be circulating to her brain if she was going to have this conversation with her mother. "A while back, yeah. He's a great guy," Shelby said. "But not someone I want to spend the rest of my life with."

She thought of Nolan. Of a guy she *could* see in her future, and wondered if she'd over-reacted earlier. If maybe the fact that she could see a future with him was making her so terrified of losing him that she was seeing cracks in the relationship where there weren't any cracks at all.

"Shelby. You know I'm not going to criticize your choices, but we both know that Alan adored you."

"I guess so," she said. "But I didn't adore him."

There was a pause, and then her mom said, "I see. And is there someone else you're seeing?"

Shelby loved her mom, but for a woman who lived by math and numbers, she was very rarely direct and straightforward in life stuff. "If you've been taking to Alan, you know there is."

She could practically hear her mother's frown. "Alan didn't know who'd captured your interest."

"His name's Nolan Wood. He's a radio host."

"What? Like a DJ?"

"It's a lot more than that, Mom. He's practically a stand-up comic."

"I'm really not sure that makes it better. You have professional appearances to think of. Does he—"

"That reminds me," she said, grateful to have a way to change the subject. "I got a call from the Young Professionals. You know, that networking and educational group? They asked me if I'd do an on-camera interview for their webpage. It will be on Facebook and YouTube and I don't know what else."

"Sweetheart, that's wonderful. That's exactly the kind of thing you should be doing."

Unlike Nolan, which wasn't.

Her mom didn't say the last, of course, but Shelby heard it anyway, and the censure was still ringing in her ears after she ended the call.

But all it did was bring her thoughts of Nolan front and center.

She reached for her phone to call him, but pulled her hand back, afraid he'd hang up on her. More than that, afraid that she would deserve it if he did.

Instead, she grabbed the copy of *Watchmen* off the

table, settled back on the love seat, and picked up where she left off.

When she finally closed the book, it was late. She'd been absorbed in the story of the flawed and fascinating heroes. A lot of times, they'd made the wrong choices, but that didn't mean she stopped rooting for them.

Then again maybe it was Nolan she was thinking of, and not the Watchmen at all.

Frowning at her own meandering thoughts, she got up and went to the bedroom, intending to go to bed. Instead, she found herself pulling on shorts and a T-shirt, grabbing her purse, and then heading out to her car.

Chapter Fifteen

CONSIDERING Nolan usually crashed early during the week so that he wasn't a zombie on his show, he very rarely went to bed before one or two a.m. on Friday and Saturday. Why would he? Those were the only days he could enjoy all the magic of late nights. Like really bad YouTube movies and obnoxious shopping networks. Both of which never failed to provide Nolan with plenty of material for his own show.

Today, he'd crashed early. A cop-out, because he didn't want to think about what Shelby had said. About him keeping part of himself from her. It was bullshit, of course. Just because he didn't catalogue every tiny aspect of himself didn't mean he was holding back on their relationship. And, honestly, what did it matter to them as a couple if he struggled with reading?

Not a goddamn thing.

All of which was a perfectly sound argument. Except for the minor flaw of being entirely unbelievable.

In other words, Nolan had spent his Saturday evening mostly alone and kicking himself for not telling the only woman he'd ever actually wanted a relationship with that he was sorry. That he'd been wrong. And that he not only should have told her about the benefit, but he should have told her the entire story about his childhood, his dyslexia, and the way he now coped as an adult.

Instead, he'd turned pissy and marched out.

Way to man up, asshole.

He rolled over in bed, craving the oblivion of sleep, but that wasn't happening. Instead he tossed and turned until he finally got up, thinking that maybe a Scotch and one of the news channels would lull him to sleep.

He'd just tossed back his first drink and was pouring the second when his doorbell chimed, which wasn't a usual occurrence since he lived in a security building, and no one other than residents could get to his door without the access code for the elevator.

He pulled a ratty robe over his boxers and *Mornings With Wood* T-shirt, then headed barefoot toward the door. It was already after midnight, and he frowned, hoping there wasn't trouble in the building. Maybe one of his neighbors had locked themselves out and needed to borrow his phone.

But when he looked through the door, it wasn't a neighbor. It was Shelby. And the relief that washed over him almost swept him away.

He unlocked the door, then yanked it open. "I'm sorry," he said as she spoke the exact same words at the exact same time.

They looked at each other, then laughed.

"How did you get up here?" he asked, after he'd hustled her inside. They usually stayed at her place since his was a studio and was furnished with garage sale rejects and IKEA pieces. He kept meaning to hire a decorator, but somehow never got around to it.

"I watched you punch in the access code the last time you brought me up. I have a good memory for numbers," she added with a wink.

Silence settled in then, and they stood awkwardly for a moment. At least it felt awkward, because he wanted to tell her everything, but didn't know where to begin.

"Listen," she said, letting him off the hook, "I appreciate your apology, really. But I'm the one who needs to do a *mea culpa*."

"No," he said firmly. "You were right. It's just that I've never talked to anyone about it except my sister. Not even my parents."

"And you don't have to talk to me."

"Yeah, I do."

She tilted her head, studying him, her serious

expression contrasted by her casual summer clothes. "Why?"

"Because I want you to know me. Hell, Shelby, you're probably the first woman I've ever wanted to know me, and that includes the woman I used to be married to."

"Oh." She said nothing else, but from the sparkle in her fascinating eyes, he could tell she was pleased.

"You wanna take a walk?"

If the non sequitur bothered her, she didn't show it. "Sure."

He disappeared into the bathroom long enough to throw on some khaki shorts over his boxers. Then they headed down to street level and started meandering toward the river in silence. When they reached Cesar Chavez, the street that ran parallel to the river, they crossed at the light, then followed the hike & bike trail under the Congress Avenue bridge and toward the grounds behind the Four Seasons hotel.

It wasn't until he drew her to a stop at a small bench by the water's edge that he started talking. But as soon as he did, the words spilled out. He told her about his struggles in school—and how even though he knew he wasn't reading "right," that he didn't ask for help because of his father. "Not Huey. He's my stepfather, and he's great. But my dad's got his own views of perfection, and a son with a dyslexia diagnosis wasn't going to hack it."

"You lived with him?"

"Half and half. And I could have told my mom the truth, but back then, my dad's attitude colored what I thought of myself. There was another kid in our neighborhood who had trouble reading, and every time my dad talked about it, he complained that the kid was stupid or lazy."

"That's horrible."

"You're not wrong. But I was young and didn't know any better. So instead of asking for help—or getting myself in a position where a teacher might realize I needed help—I started learning to cope. I became the class clown. I developed a fucking awesome memory. I learned to fight my way through a word, then a sentence, then a book if I had enough time—so multiple choice tests worked okay for me. Essays, not so much."

"And nobody noticed."

"In elementary and middle school? Not even. In high school, they started. But I dove into extracurriculars—especially speech and drama—and anyone who noticed the dip in my grades wrote it down to me being overextended."

"Don't drama and speech involve a lot of reading?"

"A lot of memorizing," he said. "I'd go slow, read into a tape recorder. After that, I just listened and memorized. I nailed my lines every time."

"But you ended up dropping out, right?"

"Funny thing about high school. Eventually they

make you write essays and research papers. I was popular as the class clown with the okay grades who had the lead in a few plays. And I wanted to go out on a high note. Not as the obnoxious kid who failed all his classes."

"Nolan…"

"It's not so bad. By that time I knew I wanted to be in radio. So I pushed that dream. And I've gotten to exactly where I want to be."

He told her more about how he'd worked his way up the ladder and about how Connor helped by giving him oral briefings.

"Does he know about the dyslexia?"

"I don't know. I've never asked. If he does, it doesn't bother him, and that's good enough for me."

"And I guess Lauren had issues."

"I never told her. She just thought I was lazy. Didn't apply myself. She never considered that by starting low in radio and working my way up I gave myself a better understanding of everything that went on. Or that I didn't go back for my GED because I reached a point where I didn't need it. And as for ambition, being happy wasn't enough for her—not that we were, but so long as we were living frugally, she would never have been satisfied. She wanted wealth, and she wanted it right then. And the fact that I've been saving since I was fourteen and have a tidy sum put away didn't impress her at all."

"Well, I'm impressed. And as an accountant, that's saying a lot."

He grinned, her words easing the unpleasant memories. "She always made me feel like I couldn't make it. And I think I was starting to believe her, because I've had a similar voice in my head—my father's—my whole life."

He exhaled. "Sometimes I wonder if I should have stayed in school. Harassed the counselor until they got me into a program, and just sucked it up when my dad belittled me."

"No," she said firmly. "No regrets, okay? Because your past made you who you are. And the Nolan I'm sitting here with is pretty terrific."

"Baby…" He cupped her head, then kissed her so tenderly it made his heart ache. When he pulled back, he lost himself in her eyes as he brushed the hair off her face with his fingertips. "Do you want to go back?"

He wanted her—God he always wanted her—and if she wanted to head back to his bed, then he wouldn't hesitate. But right then, he only really wanted to hold her.

"Do you mind if we stay here for a while? I just want to watch the river and be with you."

"Sweetheart, that sounds perfect to me."

HE THOUGHT about that night at the river days later as he stood in a tuxedo behind a podium in the ballroom at the Westin Hotel in North Austin. The huge room was full of round tables, each of which sat eight guests. And every table was full, as the staff had told him they would be when they'd called last week to give him an update on the event.

Normally, Nolan had no problem talking to crowds. After all, he did it every day at work, although those listeners were blissfully invisible to him.

Still, he'd never even hiccupped at a public appearance, because that was all about being Nolan Wood the celebrity. Pop on the schtick, and away you go.

Today, he was being himself. And that was infinitely harder.

He'd been a nervous wreck getting dressed at Shelby's house, so much so that she'd had to deal with his bowtie. He'd calmed himself by watching her dress in a stunning red number that she told him she'd borrowed from her friend Hannah.

"Why bother?" he'd asked when she'd put on a lacy thong. "Go commando. You're practically naked under there, anyway."

"You're insane. It's a gala benefit. For kids."

"I don't think kids are coming to the gala. And even if they do, they won't be peeking under your dress."

"I'm not ditching the underwear."

"Not even if it calms my nerves?"

But she simply gave him a hard stare as she shimmied into the dress, then slipped on her shoes. "Not even," she said. "Besides, they say nerves are good before a speech. Gives you that extra adrenalin kick. So you're welcome."

He'd laughed then. Now, he allowed himself only a tiny smile, letting the memory settle his nerves once again. And then, as the room calmed, he began to talk.

When he'd planned his speech, he realized that a lot of what wanted to include tracked what he'd told Shelby during their night by the river. He talked about his past, about his struggles, about his secrets and his shame, and that was what he now told the folks in this ballroom.

He'd told his parents the full truth three days before, and now they were watching him with so much pride it made his throat thick. Amanda sat beside them, positively beaming, and Shelby was next to her, having abandoned her table for his under the pretense of chatting up Amanda about accounting work for her real estate company. They'd spent much of the evening together, and he'd been relieved to see how well they got along. Not that he'd doubted it, but memories of Amanda and Lauren's mutual disdain still lingered.

As he continued his speech, he was surprised to see tears in the eyes of many in the audience. Considering he was used to making people laugh, the impact of his words was humbling.

And when he finally wrapped and stepped off the podium, he had so many hands to shake and good wishes to receive, that it took a full forty-five minutes before he finally manage to end up alone with Shelby.

"You were great," she said.

"Take off your panties," he countered, making her laugh and almost spit out the wine she'd just sipped.

"One track mind, much?"

"Hey, I'm like a god here. Did you see the reaction?"

From the way she beamed at him, he knew that she had. "Your excellent performance here doesn't earn you a naughty fantasy."

"Fantasies I can manage on my own. I want the reality."

She rose up on her toes, then kissed his cheek. "No. But I'm incredibly proud of you."

"And yet you still won't get naked under that dress."

She lifted a shoulder, her expression just a little wicked. "Take me home," she said, "and I'll get as naked as you want."

"Sweetheart, you've got yourself a deal."

Chapter Sixteen

SHELBY ALWAYS KNEW that she liked routines. It went along with liking numbers and the way they made sense and followed patterns. But she'd never imagined just how comfortable it would be to slide into a routine with a man.

Then again, she'd never imagined Nolan.

When she thought about it logically, they didn't fit at all. Her, all ordered and precise. Him, practically overflowing with wild and untamed energy.

But that was surface stuff. Underneath, they fit. Not because they were alike, but because they were like a jigsaw puzzle. Their differences meshed perfectly, and once together, everything made sense.

"Penny for your thoughts," he said, coming into the living room with two cups of coffee. Since his speech, he'd pretty much moved into her place. He even had his very own drawer. And Shelby loved the domesticity of it.

"Are you only worth a penny?" she asked lifting her feet so he could sit, then replacing them in his lap. "Because I was thinking of you."

"Then we're even, because I'm always thinking of you."

"We are so sappy," she said, then laughed.

"I won't tell if you won't."

"Deal."

He glanced at his wristwatch. "I need to get going. You'll come later?"

"I wish I could come now." Tonight was the Mr. March contest at The Fix, and Nolan was going in early to meet with everyone involved since he was ramping up the promo for The Fix on his show.

"I'll probably be late," she reminded him. She gestured toward the stacks of paper on her coffee table. All minor crises that had to be dealt with, and so she'd brought the work home so that she could focus properly. "And then I have to meet Frank after work and brief him."

"But even if you don't make the contest, you'll meet me there?"

"Absolutely," she said. "And as for the contest, I still think you should enter."

"Too late now."

"Not for Mr. April."

He narrowed his eyes. "Not happening."

"If I can surprise you, can that be my prize?"

"Surprise me?"

"Yeah, you know. Pull a rabbit out of a hat. Give you a blowjob while we're doing eighty on the toll-road. Stuff like that."

"Let's skip that one."

"Illustrative purposes only," she promised. "But if I manage a safe surprise…"

"I guess it'll depend on the surprise."

She rolled her eyes, but knew it was the best she'd get from him. "Go," she said. "And let me get back to work."

It really did take her all afternoon and into the early evening to get a handle on her various projects, but that still left her plenty of time to get to The Fix and settle in. Because she had no meeting tonight. She just needed to go alone. Because that was all part of her plan.

NOLAN CLAPPED Cam on the shoulder, congratulated him on being Mr. March, and thanked him for doing the promo spot. Then Cam pretty much bolted. Not that Nolan could blame him. Nolan knew damn well that the only thing on Cam's mind at the moment was Mina.

He checked his watch, then glanced again at the door. He still hadn't seen Shelby come in, and he hoped that he hadn't missed her in the crowd. He'd been to all three of the Man of the Month contests, and with each event the crowd grew bigger and bigger, such that Brent was going to have to hire extra security to make sure the crowd didn't get too rowdy and that the door didn't let too many people in and violate the fire code.

But, again, that was something Nolan didn't care about.

He wanted Shelby, and he was about to pull out his phone and text her when Aly hurried up, her expression harried and her tray overfull. "A lady just tipped me twenty to make sure this gets to you," she said, then shoved a folded receipt into his hand. He started to ask if she'd given him the wrong thing when he realized that the handwriting on the thin strip of paper was more than just a signature.

He unfolded it, then laughed out loud at the note in Shelby's neat, precise handwriting—*Surprise*.

As soon as his laugh faded, though, he frowned. What was the surprise? For that matter, where was Shelby?

The question was answered almost the instant he'd asked it. Because there she was, walking toward him in her familiar linen blend suit skirt and matching suit jacket. That, however, was the end of familiar. Her usual buttoned-to-the-collar shirt was open all the way to her cleavage, revealing the white lace trim of what was undoubtedly a sexy camisole.

And most interesting of all, she was walking on the same incredibly high fuck-me pumps she'd been wearing the night he'd first laid eyes on her.

"Shel? What is it?" he asked as she approached. "Are you okay?"

As soon as the words were out of his mouth, he kicked himself, because of course she was okay. *He* was the one having heart palpitations.

"I'm fine," she purred. "I have something for you."

She reached into her purse, and then pressed something soft into his hand before flashing him a flirty smile and continuing on toward the exit.

He watched her go for a full minute before thinking to look down into his hand. When he did, he felt his cock grow hard. Because he was holding a pair of red *La Perla* panties—and he was quite certain that his Paradox—who had repeatedly refused to go commando—was wearing absolutely nothing at all.

SHELBY KEPT WALKING EVEN though she knew that she had Nolan's attention. And sure enough, she heard his footsteps hurrying to catch up to her. She glanced over her shoulder as she walked, lifted her brows, and said, "Good surprise?"

"Very. But where are you going?"

She paused long enough to look him up and

down, lingering her gaze in the vicinity of his cock. "I thought we'd go to your place. Walking distance, right?"

His mouth curved up. "It most certainly is. And we can take the shortcut."

Her pulse picked up tempo at the idea of getting naked with him sooner. "I'm game," she said. "Lead the way."

He stepped beside her, then took her hand as he led her through an alley behind the Bank of America building.

"How is this faster?" she asked, and he laughed.

"I didn't say a shortcut to what," he said as he eased her up against the brick wall of the alley. They were hidden from view from pedestrians on both Fifth and Sixth Streets by the uneven nature of the wall and the scattered Dumpsters and metal storage containers.

"What are you doing?" she asked as he inched the skirt up, exposing her to the dim ambient light.

"What I've been wanting to do since I first tried to get those damn panties out from under your dress," he said, then lifted her up so quickly and unexpectedly she gasped.

He ordered her to hook her legs on his shoulders, and she complied, both turned on and slightly terrified of falling. But he had her fast, and she realized just how strong those muscled arms really were.

"Arch back," he ordered, and since the next thing

he did with his mouth was cover her clit and suck, she did what he said. And as he worked a beautiful magic on her sex, she opened her eyes, looked at the sky, and let Nolan hold her tight and keep her safe as he, quite literally, took her to the stars.

Chapter Seventeen

"I'M SERIOUS," Hannah said as she poured a round of Pinot Punch for the table. "Electric toothbrushes. I mean, who would have thought, right?" She rolled her eyes, then continued. "Although I guess I just lack imagination, because apparently the electric toothbrush vibrator craze is going strong. I just read this huge article online."

Shelby pressed her legs together. There'd been no vibrators last night, but abandoning her panties had definitely made for a quality evening. She remembered the way his hands had felt—not to mention the rest of him—as she caught Nolan's eye across the bar. The air crackled, and she knew his mind had traveled back with hers.

Yeah, she thought as she squeezed her legs together again. *Nice to be on the same wavelength.*

"It's getting rowdy over here," Reece said, grinning as he and Nolan came over to join the table. He put his hand on Jenna's shoulder, and she reached up to touch it. "What are you talking about?"

"Dental hygiene," Jenna said, and she, Shelby, Brooke, and Hannah melted into laughter again.

"This is that electric toothbrush thing, isn't it?" Nolan asked.

Shelby looked up at him, intrigued, while across the table Hannah murmured, "Well, well."

Nolan held his hands up in surrender. "Fodder for my show, people. Just fodder for my show." He winked at Shelby. "Unless you want it to be more," he added, and her cheeks burned so quick and so hot that she had no choice but to kick him under the table. A lame kick with no follow-through that only had him laughing.

"Nolan's entering the Mr. April contest," she announced, figuring that was punishment enough.

He sighed, but didn't argue, and she did a mental fist pump, shoring up her victory.

"Not my idea," he said, grinning at her. "I lost a bet. But the payment was worth it."

"It's all good," Reece said. "Good promo for the bar and for your show. Honestly, we can't lose."

"No," Nolan said, his gaze burning into Shelby, "you're right. I definitely feel like a winner lately."

"HEY, MOM," Shelby said as she punched the button to accept the incoming call through her car's audio system. "What's up?" Shelby knew her voice sounded rattled, but it had been a crazy week at work, and now she was on her way to being late for the Young Professionals taping.

It would have been smarter to let her mom go straight to voicemail. The last time she'd talked to her mother, she'd been less than excited about Shelby dating Nolan. And today of all days, Shelby didn't need anything negative in her head.

"I'm on my way to that Young Professionals thing I mentioned last week," Shelby added, hoping her mom would understand that this was not the moment to mess with her daughter's head.

"You'll do great, sweetheart. No, I just called to let you know that I listened to Nolan's show this morning."

Shelby's hands tensed on the steering wheel as she waited for her mom to continue, but the silence lingered for so long she was afraid the call dropped. "Mom? Are you there? What did you think?"

Mentally, she banged her head against the steering wheel. Considering Nolan's usual routine, that was really not a question she ought to be asking her mom. Ever.

But especially not today.

"Well, honestly, I wish I'd realized how, um, racy it

is. I wouldn't have listened with your father in the car."

"I didn't listen this morning," Shelby admitted, her stomach twisting a little. Surely the one time her parents listened wasn't a time when Nolan went even more over the top. Was it? "I was prepping for a client meeting and this interview. But what did he say?"

"Oh, it was funny," her mother said, but entirely lacking in conviction. "Just … raw. All about toothbrushes and electric shavers and—"

"Oh, God." Shelby was going to kill Hannah for ever bringing that up. *Honestly.*

"Well, that was my reaction, too."

Shelby winced; she hadn't meant to say that out loud. "It's his brand, Mom. He does a raunchy morning show. It gets the audience going, makes drive time more fun."

"Hmm."

Shelby squirmed as her underarms started to sweat from nerves—and not nervousness about the upcoming show. "Listen, I need to go. I have to do this interview, and—"

"I know. I just worry. Alan was so devastated when you turned him down, and now you seem to have gone a little off the rails. I mean, these stories Nolan tells about him and this Paradox woman—that's just him making up vulgar stories for his audience, I assume? I mean, Shelby, he's not talking about the two of you, is he?"

"Mom, I don't even know what stories you're talking about." Which was *so* not an answer, but maybe her mother with her genius level IQ, multiple degrees, and MENSA membership wouldn't notice the obfuscation. "Listen, I'm almost to the library and I want to listen to some meditation tapes before the interview. Clear my head the way you told me to that time, remember?"

"Right. Of course. Good luck. You're going to do great." She'd half-expected her mother to insist they finish the Nolan-track of the conversation, but she should have known better. Her mom would never mess with her head before a professional event. Not on purpose, anyway.

As for Shelby having a great interview, she hoped her mother was right, but as she turned into the library parking lot and hurried to the community room that the organization had booked for the interview, she had a sinking feeling that her day was cursed.

The room was set up like a classroom, with two empty chairs for the speakers at the front, and rows of already-occupied chairs for the audience. The camera stood on a tripod in the middle of the aisle and focused only on the two chairs where Shelby and the host would be sitting.

"Hi!" A short woman with dark curly hair and a bright smile hurried over. "I'm Melanie. We talked on the phone."

"Great to meet you."

"Do you need some water? We'd like to start right on time. The library has something following us this week and they want us out exactly at a quarter 'til."

"That's fine," Shel said, and the woman walked her through how the session would go. Intro. Chat. Q&A. Conclusion.

"Easy enough, right?" Melanie asked, and Shelby nodded, hoping it was as easy as it sounded and trying to ignore the portents of doom that had gathered in the car. Soon enough, they were settled, the camera was rolling, and Melanie was diving in.

"Good afternoon and welcome to Young Professionals Chat. I'm your host Melanie Hancock. For those of you just now discovering this channel, we're a social media education and networking resource for young professionals, just like our name suggests. Our interviews stream live, but you can always find video at our website."

She smiled broadly, then continued. "Today, we're talking to Shelby Drake, a certified public accountant who works in consulting and client management at Brandywine Financial Consulting here in Austin. Shelby, thanks so much for joining us."

"Happy to be here."

"You took the CPA exam relatively young. Can you tell us about that?"

As soon as the question was out, Shelby realized

her worries were unfounded. She could talk about being a CPA until the end of time.

Melanie continued. "A lot of our viewers are college students still trying to decide on a career, so we like to talk with our guests about both the work and play aspects of their lives. I imagine a high pressure job like that means that you have a limited social life."

"Well, accounting tends to come in waves, with the most crazy times being around tax season. And that's often true even if you're doing work that doesn't specifically entail filing tax returns for your clients. But because of those built in highs and lows, there are periods where evenings and weekends are reasonably free."

"Now, you're not married, so I'm going to assume that you date. Do you tend to date within the profession?"

"Oh, not necessarily." There was really no reason for trepidation, but Shelby had the strangest sense that the chat was about to go off the rails.

"Are you seeing anyone in particular?"

"Um, well, that's—I mean, I'm not sure how I feel about getting that specific on a live show."

"Understandable. But we're really interested in how a professional like yourself deals with things like client relations if his or her partner has a job or a personality that lacks a certain decorum."

Her mouth went dry. "I'm not sure I know what you mean."

"Well, you and Nolan Wood have been seen together a few times, and I believe he escorted you to the DTRR benefit recently. And anyone who's lived in Austin for more than five minutes knows that his show can get a little raunchy. The name of the show itself is a double entendre, *Mornings With Wood.*"

"I don't think any of my clients judge me by my friends. And I'd say most of my clients have a good sense of humor, too."

"But what if you and Mr. Wood were dating?"

"You want me to discuss hypotheticals? I didn't think this was that kind of program."

"It's a program for helping young people navigate professional pitfalls. I hope you don't think we're crossing a line, but since the rumors are that you're dating Nolan Wood—and since you're a professional woman with some very conservative clients—we're wondering how you separate, from a professional point of view—your work life from your private life, especially when it crosses into his and into the public."

"I—" She had no idea how to answer. Worse, all she wanted to do was bolt.

"Like this morning's episode, for example. He did a whole schtick on toothbrushes as vibrators. And when..."

Melanie's words faded out, overpowered by the memory of the disgust in her mother's voice when she talked about this morning's program. And the memory of just how racy last night's conversation at The Fix had become.

"I'm sorry," she blurted, interrupting Melanie. "Maybe you're trying to skew this program toward a tabloid audience and you're using me to do it, but I really can't speak to the subject. Nolan and I are friends. That's all." Not true, but also not Melanie's business. "And," she added, rising to her feet, "I think we're done."

She walked calmly out, knowing damn well she was still on camera. And though her shirt was damp with nervous sweat, she felt pretty damn ballsy for sticking up for herself.

That feeling vanished the moment she got home, intending to change her sweat-stained blouse before heading back into the office. Something was off. Just slightly askew. It took her a second to realize that the sweat jacket Nolan had left draped over the arm of her love seat was gone.

Not exactly a portent of doom, but seeing—or rather *not* seeing—sent apprehension flooding through her.

"Nolan?"

No answer. Not that she expected one. He should still be at the studio, prepping for the next day's show. She headed back to the bedroom, ostensibly to change shirts, but really because she hoped he'd be back there, sitting on the bed waiting for her.

He wasn't. But the drawer he used was open and

empty a single sheet of white paper was on the bed, a message written in Nolan's choppy scrawl.

Heard the show.

Need some time.

N.

Chapter Eighteen

SHELBY BENT over the toilet and dry-heaved for what had to be the fifteenth time, but her stomach wouldn't calm down. Her body felt hot, then cold. Her skin clammy.

This wasn't illness, though. This was terror.

She'd lost him.

How could she have been so stupid? So insensitive?

How could she have ever, *ever,* said something to make him think she didn't want him.

She did.

Dear God, how she did.

But she'd felt trapped. Closed in. Downright scared. Because how could she—her of all people— live in that spotlight that he did? And not just any spotlight, but a downright raunchy one.

Surely he understood that. He knew her, after all.

He had to know that her reaction wasn't about him. It was about standing in that spotlight where people like her mother would see her and frown and wag judgmental fingers.

That's what she was scared of.

Not Nolan. Because how could she ever be scared of the man she loved?

"YOU REALLY OUGHT to take her calls, dude," Connor said as they sat in the KIKX break room after the show. "She's been calling every day like clockwork."

"Maybe I should," Nolan said. "Hell, maybe I deserved it. Maybe she's right to be embarrassed by me."

"Bullshit," Connor said. "I mean, come on, man. You make people laugh. You make people think. You damn sure make people talk, and that's a good thing."

"I don't know. Maybe. I only—"

The intercom buzzed and the receptionist announced a call from Amanda.

"I'll take it in here," he told her, then went to the phone and punched the button for the proper line.

Connor stood and walked to the door, signaling that he'd catch him later.

"Amanda? What's up?"

"It's me," Shelby said. "I figured you'd talk to Amanda, but please, don't hang up."

Surprisingly, he didn't. The phone was still to his ear. And as hurt and as angry as he was, the sound of her voice only underscored how damn much he missed her.

But missing her wasn't enough. Not by a long shot.

"You haven't returned any of my calls," she said.

"There's nothing to say. I've been in a relationship with a woman who didn't respect me. I'm not going there again."

"No. No, don't you dare lump me in with Lauren. I respect you, Nolan. Hell, I need you. I was just caught off guard. Scared."

"About what?"

"Being caught in the spotlight like that. With my mother freaking out about toothbrush vibrators and people asking me about the stuff between us that you talk about on your show. I can't riff about sex like you can. And I'm not comfortable with people looking that closely at my life, much less my sex life. But it's not *you*. Don't you get it? Don't you understand the difference?"

"Baby," he said softly, his heart squeezing tight in defense against the words he had to say. Because even though she didn't realize it, she'd just told him that there was no way for them to be together. Not ever. "I do. I get it."

"Well?"

"Don't you see, Shelby? That's the life you'd have. We can't be together behind concrete walls. If you're with me the walls are glass. I can shield you some, but not completely. Because even if I don't talk about our sex life, I'll still be talking about vibrators and hard-ons, and your mother will be mortified and your clients will raise their eyebrows. It's the one constant of what I do, and there's no way around it. And we both know I can't quit. It's what I am. It's who I am."

"I know." He heard the small sob and it nearly broke his heart.

"It can't work, Shelby. And you're the one who just told us why."

FOR DAYS, Shelby battled her thoughts, trying to decide what to do. And trying to figure out who she was, and what she wanted.

All she knew for certain was that she wanted Nolan. What she didn't know was what she was willing to give up. Or, for that matter, how to convince him.

The answer to the first question came to her on Wednesday after work when Frank called her into his office and told her that a local radio station, KIKX, was looking to hire a consulting accountant for a long-term project.

"It's just the right kind of client and the right type of work to get you squarely on partnership track."

It was, too. That job would probably seal her fate, and she'd be a partner within the next two years.

She turned it down. Because the only thing she could think about was the no-dating policy between Brandywine employees and the employees of clients. And the thought of not being with Nolan for that long was impossible to bear.

Which told her what she was willing to give up.

Now she just had to figure out how to get him back. And when she realized that it was Wednesday evening and the night of the Mr. April contest, the pieces fell into place.

Shelby knew exactly what to do.

She just hoped it would work.

BY THE TIME Shelby reached the bar, the contest was already underway, and she saw Nolan standing shirtless on stage as the final guy walked to the microphone, flexed his muscles, and told the audience to vote for him.

As he walked back to stand in the line with the other men, Beverly Martin, a local film actress who was the contest's emcee, started for the mike, presumably to wrap up the contest and tell the audience to cast their votes.

"*Wait*," Shelby called, sprinting for the stairs that led up to the stage.

Beverly took a step back, clearly confused, as Shelby bounded onto the stage and grabbed the mike.

"It's okay!" A voice shouted from the back of the room, and Shelby said a silent thank you that Brooke had gotten her text message begging her to please ask Jenna to let Shelby have this moment in the spotlight.

Now that she was here, though, staring at hundreds of faces, she thought she just might die of mortification.

Swallowing, she turned to look behind her, needing to see Nolan. He stood shirtless with the other guys, his eyes wide, and his weight shifted forward, as if he was ready to leap to her rescue.

And that alone gave her the courage to go on.

"Um, hi. So, right. I realize this is a little over the top, but I just wanted to tell you why you should vote for Nolan Wood."

Behind her, all the guys started to mumble, and someone from the audience shouted, "Anything for a rating, Wood! Awesome stunt!"

"No, it's not a stunt. I mean, I guess it is. But it's not his stunt. It's mine. And it's not for ratings." She looked over her shoulder at Nolan, then bit her lip before continuing. "I've got a much bigger prize in mind.

"So, right, moving on. Why vote for him? Well, his abs are awesome and he's a really good kisser."

"Jesus, Shelby," Nolan murmured, which only made her laugh nervously and continue. "But all these guys look pretty awesome. So it has to be about more than that. And the thing is, Nolan's got this great way of looking at life. He embraces passion and silliness. And he sees sex—oh, God—here I go, talking about sex in front of all you people—but he sees it in all its incarnations. A covenant, a promise, an escapade. Fun. Silly. Reverent."

She drew in a breath and plowed on, afraid that if she paused, they'd kick her off the stage. "He's a guy who serves the community in so many ways. And he's a guy who really lives in it. A guy who truly made himself. A man who's so comfortable in his own skin he's willing to put all of himself out in front of the world. And that's something I really admire.

"The thing is, I'm not like that. I don't have that openness, and that scared me, and I screwed up. But that was my bad. Not his. Because Nolan is the best man I know, and I'm telling you this so that you'll vote for him. But hands off, girls, because he's mine. And when he talks about his Paradox on the radio, just so you know, that's me, and I loved every minute I had with him."

She wiped away a tear. "Hopefully I'll have more, but I'm so afraid that I lost him. And I really hope I didn't. Because I'm head over heels in love with him."

She stood for a second, and the room was totally and completely silent. Then she managed a tiny smile and said, "Ah, um, I should go," and started toward the stairs.

She didn't make it. Someone had her arm, and when she looked back, she saw that it was Nolan.

She only had time to gasp before he pulled her close, then bent her body back in a full-on Hollywood pose. He kissed her then, long and deep and wonderful, and when he put her back on her feet, her whole body was shaking.

"I love you," he said, and she burst into tears.

"I said it first," she managed, gulping a little.

"Yeah, you did." He pushed the hair off her face. "Let's get out of here."

"They haven't announced the winner yet."

He looked out at the audience, then to the other men. Then he looked at her face and his eyes locked on hers. "Trust me," he said. "I just won the only thing I want."

Epilogue

TYREE JOHNSON LEANED against the oak bar and watched as Nolan and Shelby headed for the door. He wondered if he should tell them to stay a bit, since in about three minutes, Beverly would announce that Nolan had won the title of Mr. April.

But he decided not to. There'd be plenty of celebrating without the boy around, and from the look on Nolan's face, wild horses couldn't keep him inside the bar.

And about damn time, Tyree thought. There wasn't much around The Fix he didn't notice, and he'd seen the two of them flirting back in April. He'd known then and there that they'd end up together. He just hadn't expected it would take months for the two of them to figure it out for themselves.

With a sigh, he started to make the circle, shaking hands and chatting up the customers. It would be a damn shame if he couldn't manage to keep The Fix open, because from the looks of it, his little bar was turning into one hell of a matchmaker's paradise.

He paused for a moment when Brent called his name, and he turned back to see his friend and partner signal for Tyree to reboot the security cameras. He flashed a thumbs-up and was about to head to the office to deal with that errand when he saw a familiar young woman.

She was tall, probably five foot eight, with skin as dark as Tyree's and a wide, easy smile that reminded him of Eva's. He'd seen her at least once before in the bar—two, maybe three days ago—and it had been that resemblance that had caught his eye. He'd seen that smile from across the bar, and it had felt like he'd taken shrapnel in the gut.

Tonight, he was more prepared, and he took a closer look at her face, realizing as he did that it wasn't just the smile that reminded him of his first love, but her huge wide-eyes and sculpted cheekbones as well.

Christ, he was a glutton for punishment. He should have just turned away the minute he saw her walk through that door. He had no idea who she was, but a storm of bittersweet memories had swept in through the door with her, twisting up his insides and making him ache with the pain of long ago losses.

Once in his office, he rebooted the security system, then sat at his desk. He knew he should either be out on the floor or taking care of the shit-ton of paperwork that came with running a bar. Instead, he reached down and opened the bottom drawer of his desk, then pulled out the battered cigar box.

He opened it, pulled out a stack of photographs, then reverently thumbed through it. Him and Teiko, his late wife. His son, Elijah, at birth. Then himself at nine years old, standing tall and trying to hold it together at his mother's funeral.

Tyree drew a shaky breath, then ran his thumb under his eyes before continuing down memory lane. There was a photo of him and Charlie Walker, Reece's dad. And one of him with Reece's uncle, Vincent, just days before he'd been mortally wounded by enemy fire in Afghanistan, then died in Tyree's arms.

Another deep breath, and Tyree continued, finally finding the photograph he'd been looking for. Over twenty years old now, the colors had faded, so that Eva's dress looked pink rather than red, and the sky more gray than blue. But the love in her eyes was still there, and the face was still hers.

His heart twisted as he recalled their weekend together in San Diego before he'd been shipped out. They'd known each other only two short weeks, but he'd been madly in love with her.

He'd thought she'd wait, but by the time he returned, she was gone, and though he'd tried to track her down, he'd had no luck. Then he met Teiko, had fallen so damn hard, and, well, life went on. A wonderful, perfect life.

Or, at least, it had been until tragedy hit.

God, he missed his wife.

He put the picture back in the cigar box, wishing he hadn't opened those doors. Eva. Teiko. Both women he'd loved.

Both women he'd lost.

There was a sharp knock on his doorframe, and he looked up to see a ghost.

He blinked.

No, not a ghost. That wasn't Eva. Of course it wasn't. But once again he was struck stupid by the resemblance.

"Mr. Johnson?" Her voice was lyrical yet strong, and achingly familiar. "They said I could come back. I—you are Tyree Johnson, right?"

"That's me."

She drew in a breath, as if his words were a relief.

"And you lived in San Diego?"

A chill raced up his spine, and he thought of his grandmother, and the way she'd always say that a ghost had walked over his grave.

"I did. But that was a long time ago. So what can I do for you now, Miss..."

"Anderson," she said. "Elena Anderson."

Elena. Tyree frowned. That was his mother's name. And when the young woman in front of him flashed a nervous smile, it wasn't Eva he saw this time, but his mother.

"Who are you?" he asked, even though in his gut he already knew the answer.

"My mother is Eva Anderson. And I think that you're my father."

Get It On

_____

Be sure not to miss Tyree and Eva in *Get It On!*

Skillful hands. A talented tongue.
Meet Mr. May.

Fate's been messing with Army veteran Tyree Johnson. It took his buddies in combat and his wife in a
fatal car accident. But he'll be damned if he'll let Fate
take his beloved bar, The Fix on Sixth.

For years, he's avoided being Fate's whipping boy
through sheer force of will, and now every bit of his
focus is centered on saving his business. Until, that is,
the first woman who ever touched his heart walks
back into his life—along with a daughter he
never knew.

After years of loneliness, Tyree's not prepared for the way Eva's sensual curves and sharp wit still capture his heart and rekindle his senses. All he knows is that for the first time in forever, he's found a passion other than his bar. But one final twist arrives when Fate pits the bar he can't bear to lose against the woman who's stolen his heart.

He's a master at red-hot ecstasy.

The Men of Man of the Month!

Are you eager to learn which Man of the Month book features which sexy hero? Here's a handy list!

Down On Me - meet Reece
Hold On Tight - meet Spencer
Need You Now - meet Cameron
Start Me Up - meet Nolan
Get It On - meet Tyree
In Your Eyes - meet Parker
Turn Me On - meet Derek
Shake It Up - meet Landon
All Night Long - meet Easton
In Too Deep - meet Matthew
Light My Fire - meet Griffin
Walk The Line - meet Brent
&
Bar Bites: A Man of the Month Cookbook

Down On Me excerpt

Did you miss book one in the Man of the Month series? Here's an excerpt from Down On Me!

Chapter One

Reece Walker ran his palms over the slick, soapy ass of the woman in his arms and knew that he was going straight to hell.

Not because he'd slept with a woman he barely knew. Not because he'd enticed her into bed with a series of well-timed bourbons and particularly inventive half-truths. Not even because he'd lied to his best friend Brent about why Reece couldn't drive with him to the airport to pick up Jenna, the third player in their trifecta of lifelong friendship.

No, Reece was staring at the fiery pit because he was a lame, horny asshole without the balls to tell the naked beauty standing in the shower with him that she wasn't the woman he'd been thinking about for the last four hours.

And if that wasn't one of the pathways to hell, it damn sure ought to be.

He let out a sigh of frustration, and Megan tilted her head, one eyebrow rising in question as she slid her hand down to stroke his cock, which was demonstrating no guilt whatsoever about the whole going to hell issue. "Am I boring you?"

"Hardly." That, at least, was the truth. He felt like a prick, yes. But he was a well-satisfied one. "I was just thinking that you're beautiful."

She smiled, looking both shy and pleased—and Reece felt even more like a heel. What the devil was wrong with him? She *was* beautiful. And hot and funny and easy to talk to. Not to mention good in bed.

But she wasn't Jenna, which was a ridiculous comparison. Because Megan qualified as fair game, whereas Jenna was one of his two best friends. She trusted him. Loved him. And despite the way his cock perked up at the thought of doing all sorts of delicious things with her in bed, Reece knew damn well that would never happen. No way was he risking their friendship. Besides, Jenna didn't love him like that. Never had, never would.

And that—plus about a billion more reasons— meant that Jenna was entirely off-limits.

Too bad his vivid imagination hadn't yet gotten the memo.

Fuck it.

He tightened his grip, squeezing Megan's perfect rear. "Forget the shower," he murmured. "I'm taking you back to bed." He needed this. Wild. Hot. Demanding. And dirty enough to keep him from thinking.

Hell, he'd scorch the earth if that's what it took to burn Jenna from his mind—and he'd leave Megan limp, whimpering, and very, very satisfied. His guilt. Her pleasure. At least it would be a win for one of them.

And who knows? Maybe he'd manage to fuck the fantasies of his best friend right out of his head.

It didn't work.

Reece sprawled on his back, eyes closed, as Megan's gentle fingers traced the intricate outline of the tattoos inked across his pecs and down his arms. Her touch was warm and tender, in stark contrast to the way he'd just fucked her—a little too wild, a little too hard, as if he were fighting a battle, not making love.

Well, that was true, wasn't it?

But it was a battle he'd lost. Victory would have brought oblivion. Yet here he was, a naked woman beside him, and his thoughts still on Jenna, as wild and intense and impossible as they'd been since that night eight months ago when the earth had shifted beneath him, and he'd let himself look at her as a woman and not as a friend.

One breathtaking, transformative night, and Jenna didn't even realize it. And he'd be damned if he'd ever let her figure it out.

Beside him, Megan continued her exploration, one fingertip tracing the outline of a star. "No names? No wife or girlfriend's initials hidden in the design?"

He turned his head sharply, and she burst out laughing.

"Oh, don't look at me like that." She pulled the sheet up to cover her breasts as she rose to her knees beside him. "I'm just making conversation. No hidden agenda at all. Believe me, the last thing I'm interested in is a relationship." She scooted away, then sat on the edge of the bed, giving him an enticing view of her bare back. "I don't even do overnights."

As if to prove her point, she bent over, grabbed her bra off the floor, and started getting dressed.

"Then that's one more thing we have in common." He pushed himself up, rested his back against the headboard, and enjoyed the view as she wiggled into her jeans.

"Good," she said, with such force that he knew she meant it, and for a moment he wondered what had soured her on relationships.

As for himself, he hadn't soured so much as fizzled. He'd had a few serious girlfriends over the years, but it never worked out. No matter how good it started, invariably the relationship crumbled. Eventually, he had to acknowledge that he simply wasn't relationship material. But that didn't mean he was a monk, the last eight months notwithstanding.

She put on her blouse and glanced around, then slipped her feet into her shoes. Taking the hint, he got up and pulled on his jeans and T-shirt. "Yes?" he asked, noticing the way she was eying him speculatively.

"The truth is, I was starting to think you might be in a relationship."

"What? Why?"

She shrugged. "You were so quiet there for a while, I wondered if maybe I'd misjudged you. I thought you might be married and feeling guilty."

Guilty.

The word rattled around in his head, and he groaned. "Yeah, you could say that."

"Oh, *hell*. Seriously?"

"No," he said hurriedly. "Not that. I'm not cheating on my non-existent wife. I wouldn't. Not ever." Not in small part because Reece wouldn't ever have a wife since he thought the institution of marriage was a crock, but he didn't see the need to explain that to Megan.

"But as for guilt?" he continued. "Yeah, tonight I've got that in spades."

She relaxed slightly. "Hmm. Well, sorry about the guilt, but I'm glad about the rest. I have rules, and I consider myself a good judge of character. It makes me cranky when I'm wrong."

"Wouldn't want to make you cranky."

"Oh, you really wouldn't. I can be a total bitch." She sat on the edge of the bed and watched as he tugged on his boots. "But if you're not hiding a wife in your attic, what are you feeling guilty about? I assure you, if it has anything to do with my satisfaction, you needn't feel guilty at all." She flashed a mischievous grin, and he couldn't help but smile back. He hadn't invited a woman into his bed for eight long months. At least he'd had the good fortune to pick one he actually liked.

"It's just that I'm a crappy friend," he admitted.

"I doubt that's true."

"Oh, it is," he assured her as he tucked his wallet into his back pocket. The irony, of course, was that as far as Jenna knew, he was an excellent friend. The best. One of her two pseudo-brothers with whom she'd sworn a blood oath the summer after sixth grade, almost twenty years ago.

From Jenna's perspective, Reece was at least as good as Brent, even if the latter scored bonus points because he was picking Jenna up at the airport while Reece was trying to fuck his personal demons into oblivion. Trying anything, in fact, that would exorcise the memory of how she'd clung to him that night, her curves enticing and her breath intoxicating, and not just because of the scent of too much alcohol.

She'd trusted him to be the white knight, her noble rescuer, and all he'd been able to think about was the feel of her body, soft and warm against his, as he carried her up the stairs to her apartment.

A wild craving had hit him that night, like a tidal wave of emotion crashing over him, washing away the outer shell of friendship and leaving nothing but raw desire and a longing so potent it nearly brought him to his knees.

It had taken all his strength to keep his distance when the only thing he'd wanted was to cover every inch of her naked body with kisses. To stroke her skin and watch her writhe with pleasure.

He'd won a hard-fought battle when he reined in his desire that night. But his victory wasn't without its wounds. She'd pierced his heart when she'd drifted to sleep in his arms, whispering that she loved him—and he knew that she meant it only as a friend.

More than that, he knew that he was the biggest asshole to ever walk the earth.

Thankfully, Jenna remembered nothing of that night. The liquor had stolen her memories, leaving her with a monster hangover, and him with a Jenna-shaped hole in his heart.

"Well?" Megan pressed. "Are you going to tell me? Or do I have to guess?"

"I blew off a friend."

"Yeah? That probably won't score you points in the Friend of the Year competition, but it doesn't sound too dire. Unless you were the best man and blew off the wedding? Left someone stranded at the side of the road somewhere in West Texas? Or promised to feed their cat and totally forgot? Oh, God. Please tell me you didn't kill Fluffy."

He bit back a laugh, feeling slightly better. "A friend came in tonight, and I feel like a complete shit for not meeting her plane."

"Well, there are taxis. And I assume she's an adult?"

"She is, and another friend is there to pick her up."

"I see," she said, and the way she slowly nodded suggested that she saw too much. "I'm guessing that *friend* means *girlfriend*? Or, no. You wouldn't do that. So she must be an ex."

"Really not," he assured her. "Just a friend. Life-long, since sixth grade."

"Oh, I get it. Longtime friend. High expectations. She's going to be pissed."

"Nah. She's cool. Besides, she knows I usually work nights."

"Then what's the problem?"

He ran his hand over his shaved head, the bristles

from the day's growth like sandpaper against his palm. "Hell if I know," he lied, then forced a smile, because whether his problem was guilt or lust or just plain stupidity, she hardly deserved to be on the receiving end of his bullshit.

He rattled his car keys. "How about I buy you one last drink before I take you home?"

"You're sure you don't mind a working drink?" Reece asked as he helped Megan out of his cherished baby blue vintage Chevy pickup. "Normally I wouldn't take you to my job, but we just hired a new bar back, and I want to see how it's going."

He'd snagged one of the coveted parking spots on Sixth Street, about a block down from The Fix, and he glanced automatically toward the bar, the glow from the windows relaxing him. He didn't own the place, but it was like a second home to him and had been for one hell of a long time.

"There's a new guy in training, and you're not there? I thought you told me you were the manager?"

"I did, and I am, but Tyree's there. The owner, I mean. He's always on site when someone new is starting. Says it's his job, not mine. Besides, Sunday's my day off, and Tyree's a stickler for keeping to the schedule."

"Okay, but why are you going then?"

"Honestly? The new guy's my cousin. He'll probably give me shit for checking in on him, but old habits die hard." Michael had been almost four when Vincent died, and the loss of his dad hit him hard. At sixteen, Reece had tried to be stoic, but Uncle Vincent had been like a second father to him, and he'd always thought of Mike as more brother than cousin. Either way, from that day on, he'd made it his job to watch out for the kid.

"Nah, he'll appreciate it," Megan said. "I've got a little sister, and she gripes when I check up on her, but it's all for show. She likes knowing I have her back. And as for getting a drink where you work, I don't mind at all."

As a general rule, late nights on Sunday were dead, both in the bar and on Sixth Street, the popular downtown Austin street that had been a focal point of the city's nightlife for decades. Tonight was no exception. At half-past one in the morning, the street was mostly deserted. Just a few cars moving slowly, their headlights shining toward the west, and a smattering of couples, stumbling and laughing. Probably tourists on their way back to one of the downtown hotels.

It was late April, though, and the spring weather was drawing both locals and tourists. Soon, the area —and the bar—would be bursting at the seams. Even on a slow Sunday night.

Situated just a few blocks down from Congress Avenue, the main downtown artery, The Fix on Sixth attracted a healthy mix of tourists and locals. The bar had existed in one form or another for decades, becoming a local staple, albeit one that had been falling deeper and deeper into disrepair until Tyree had bought the place six years ago and started it on much-needed life support.

"You've never been here before?" Reece asked as he paused in front of the oak and glass doors etched with the bar's familiar logo.

"I only moved downtown last month. I was in Los Angeles before."

The words hit Reece with unexpected force. Jenna had been in LA, and a wave of both longing and regret crashed over him. He should have gone with Brent. What the hell kind of friend was he, punishing Jenna because he couldn't control his own damn libido?

With effort, he forced the thoughts back. He'd already beaten that horse to death.

"Come on," he said, sliding one arm around her shoulder and pulling open the door with his other. "You're going to love it."

He led her inside, breathing in the familiar mix of alcohol, southern cooking, and something indiscernible he liked to think of as the scent of a damn good time. As he expected, the place was mostly empty. There was no live music on Sunday nights, and at less than an hour to closing, there were only three customers in the front room.

"Megan, meet Cameron," Reece said, pulling out a stool for her as he nodded to the bartender in introduction. Down the bar, he saw Griffin Draper, a regular, lift his head, his face obscured by his hoodie, but his attention on Megan as she chatted with Cam about the house wines.

Reece nodded hello, but Griffin turned back to his notebook so smoothly and nonchalantly that Reece wondered if maybe he'd just been staring into space, thinking, and hadn't seen Reece or Megan at all. That was probably the case, actually. Griff wrote a popular podcast that had been turned into an even more popular web series, and when he wasn't recording the dialogue, he was usually writing a script.

"So where's Mike? With Tyree?"

Cameron made a face, looking younger than his twenty-four years. "Tyree's gone."

"You're kidding. Did something happen with Mike?" His cousin was a responsible kid. Surely he hadn't somehow screwed up his first day on the job.

"No, Mike's great." Cam slid a Scotch in front of Reece. "Sharp, quick, hard worker. He went off the clock about an hour ago, though. So you just missed him."

"Tyree shortened his shift?"

Cam shrugged. "Guess so. Was he supposed to be on until closing?"

"Yeah." Reece frowned. "He was. Tyree say why he cut him loose?"

"No, but don't sweat it. Your cousin's fitting right in. Probably just because it's Sunday and slow. " He made a face. "And since Tyree followed him out, guess who's closing for the first time alone."

"So you're in the hot seat, huh? " Reece tried to sound casual. He was standing behind Megan's stool, but now he moved to lean against the bar, hoping his casual posture suggested that he wasn't worried at all. He was, but he didn't want Cam to realize it. Tyree didn't leave employees to close on their own. Not until he'd spent weeks training them.

"I told him I want the weekend assistant manager position. I'm guessing this is his way of seeing how I work under pressure."

"Probably," Reece agreed half-heartedly. "What did he say?"

"Honestly, not much. He took a call in the office, told Mike he could head home, then about fifteen minutes later said he needed to take off, too, and that I was the man for the night."

"Trouble?" Megan asked.

"No. Just chatting up my boy," Reece said, surprised at how casual his voice sounded. Because the scenario had trouble printed all over it. He just wasn't sure what kind of trouble.

He focused again on Cam. "What about the wait-staff?" Normally, Tiffany would be in the main bar taking care of the customers who sat at tables. "He didn't send them home, too, did he?"

"Oh, no," Cam said. "Tiffany and Aly are scheduled to be on until closing, and they're in the back with—"

But his last words were drowned out by a high-pitched squeal of "*You're here!*" and Reece looked up to find Jenna Montgomery—the woman he craved—barreling across the room and flinging herself into his arms.

Meet Damien Stark

Only his passion could set her free…

Release Me
Claim Me
Complete Me
Anchor Me
Lost With Me

Meet Damien Stark in Release Me, *book 1 of the wildly sensual series that's left millions of readers breathless …*

Chapter One

A cool ocean breeze caresses my bare shoulders, and I shiver, wishing I'd taken my roommate's advice and brought a shawl with me tonight. I arrived in Los Angeles only four days ago, and I haven't yet adjusted to the concept of summer temperatures changing with the setting of the sun. In Dallas, June is hot, July is hotter, and August is hell.

Not so in California, at least not by the beach. LA Lesson Number One: Always carry a sweater if you'll be out after dark.

Of course, I could leave the balcony and go back inside to the party. Mingle with the millionaires. Chat up the celebrities. Gaze dutifully at the paintings. It is a gala art opening, after all, and my boss brought me here to meet and greet and charm and chat. Not to lust over the panorama that is coming alive in front of me. Bloodred clouds bursting against the pale orange sky. Blue-gray waves shimmering with dappled gold.

I press my hands against the balcony rail and lean forward, drawn to the intense, unreachable beauty of the setting sun. I regret that I didn't bring the battered Nikon I've had since high school. Not that it would have fit in my itty-bitty beaded purse. And a bulky camera bag paired with a little black dress is a big, fat fashion no-no.

But this is my very first Pacific Ocean sunset, and I'm determined to document the moment. I pull out my iPhone and snap a picture.

"Almost makes the paintings inside seem redundant, doesn't it?" I recognize the throaty, feminine voice and turn to face Evelyn Dodge, retired actress turned agent turned patron of the arts—and my hostess for the evening.

"I'm so sorry. I know I must look like a giddy tourist, but we don't have sunsets like this in Dallas."

"Don't apologize," she says. "I pay for that view every month when I write the mortgage check. It damn well better be spectacular."

I laugh, immediately more at ease.

"Hiding out?"

"Excuse me?"

"You're Carl's new assistant, right?" she asks, referring to my boss of three days.

"Nikki Fairchild."

"I remember now. Nikki from Texas." She looks me up and down, and I wonder if she's disappointed that I don't have big hair and cowboy boots. "So who does he want you to charm?"

"Charm?" I repeat, as if I don't know exactly what she means.

She cocks a single brow. "Honey, the man would rather walk on burning coals than come to an art show. He's fishing for investors and you're the bait." She makes a rough noise in the back of her throat. "Don't worry. I won't press you to tell me who. And I don't blame you for hiding out. Carl's brilliant, but he's a bit of a prick."

"It's the brilliant part I signed on for," I say, and she barks out a laugh.

The truth is that she's right about me being the bait. "Wear a cocktail dress," Carl had said. "Something flirty."

Seriously? I mean, *Seriously?*

I should have told him to wear his own damn cocktail dress. But I didn't. Because I want this job. I fought to get this job. Carl's company, C-Squared Technologies, successfully launched three web-based products in the last eighteen months. That track record had caught the industry's eye, and Carl had been hailed as a man to watch.

More important from my perspective, that meant he was a man to learn from, and I'd prepared for the job interview with an intensity bordering on obsession. Landing the position had been a huge coup for me. So what if he wanted me to wear something flirty? It was a small price to pay.

Shit.

"I need to get back to being the bait," I say.

"Oh, hell. Now I've gone and made you feel either guilty or self-conscious. Don't be. Let them get liquored up in there first. You catch more flies with alcohol anyway. Trust me. I know."

She's holding a pack of cigarettes, and now she taps one out, then extends the pack to me. I shake my head. I love the smell of tobacco—it reminds me of my grandfather—but actually inhaling the smoke does nothing for me.

"I'm too old and set in my ways to quit," she says. "But God forbid I smoke in my own damn house. I swear, the mob would burn me in effigy. You're not going to start lecturing me on the dangers of second-hand smoke, are you?"

"No," I promise.

"Then how about a light?"

I hold up the itty-bitty purse. "One lipstick, a credit card, my driver's license, and my phone."

"No condom?"

"I didn't think it was that kind of party," I say dryly.

"I knew I liked you." She glances around the balcony. "What the hell kind of party am I throwing if I don't even have one goddamn candle on one goddamn table? Well, fuck it." She puts the unlit cigarette to her mouth and inhales, her eyes closed and her expression rapturous. I can't help but like her. She wears hardly any makeup, in stark contrast to all the other women here tonight, myself included, and her dress is more of a caftan, the batik pattern as interesting as the woman herself.

She's what my mother would call a brassy broad —loud, large, opinionated, and self-confident. My mother would hate her. I think she's awesome.

She drops the unlit cigarette onto the tile and grinds it with the toe of her shoe. Then she signals to one of the catering staff, a girl dressed all in black and carrying a tray of champagne glasses.

The girl fumbles for a minute with the sliding door that opens onto the balcony, and I imagine those flutes tumbling off, breaking against the hard tile, the scattered shards glittering like a wash of diamonds.

I picture myself bending to snatch up a broken stem. I see the raw edge cutting into the soft flesh at the base of my thumb as I squeeze. I watch myself clutching it tighter, drawing strength from the pain, the way some people might try to extract luck from a rabbit's foot.

The fantasy blurs with memory, jarring me with its potency. It's fast and powerful, and a little disturbing because I haven't needed the pain in a long time, and I don't understand why I'm thinking about it now, when I feel steady and in control.

I am fine, I think. *I am fine, I am fine, I am fine.*

"Take one, honey," Evelyn says easily, holding a flute out to me.

I hesitate, searching her face for signs that my mask has slipped and she's caught a glimpse of my rawness. But her face is clear and genial.

"No, don't you argue," she adds, misinterpreting my hesitation. "I bought a dozen cases and I hate to see good alcohol go to waste. Hell no," she adds when the girl tries to hand her a flute. "I hate the stuff. Get me a vodka. Straight up. Chilled. Four olives. Hurry up, now. Do you want me to dry up like a leaf and float away?"

The girl shakes her head, looking a bit like a twitchy, frightened rabbit. Possibly one that had sacrificed his foot for someone else's good luck.

Evelyn's attention returns to me. "So how do you like LA? What have you seen? Where have you been? Have you bought a map of the stars yet? Dear God, tell me you're not getting sucked into all that tourist bullshit."

"Mostly I've seen miles of freeway and the inside of my apartment."

"Well, that's just sad. Makes me even more glad that Carl dragged your skinny ass all the way out here tonight."

I've put on fifteen welcome pounds since the years when my mother monitored every tiny thing that went in my mouth, and while I'm perfectly happy with my size-eight ass, I wouldn't describe it as skinny. I know Evelyn means it as a compliment, though, and so I smile. "I'm glad he brought me, too. The paintings really are amazing."

"Now don't do that—don't you go sliding into the polite-conversation routine. No, no," she says before I can protest. "I'm sure you mean it. Hell, the paintings are wonderful. But you're getting the flat-eyed look of a girl on her best behavior, and we can't have that. Not when I was getting to know the real you."

"Sorry," I say. "I swear I'm not fading away on you."

Because I genuinely like her, I don't tell her that she's wrong—she hasn't met the real Nikki Fairchild. She's met Social Nikki who, much like Malibu Barbie, comes with a complete set of accessories. In my case, it's not a bikini and a convertible. Instead, I have the *Elizabeth Fairchild Guide for Social Gatherings*.

My mother's big on rules. She claims it's her Southern upbringing. In my weaker moments, I agree. Mostly, I just think she's a controlling bitch. Since the first time she took me for tea at the Mansion at Turtle Creek in Dallas at age three, I have had the rules drilled into my head. How to walk, how to talk, how to dress. What to eat, how much to drink, what kinds of jokes to tell.

I have it all down, every trick, every nuance, and I wear my practiced pageant smile like armor against the world. The result being that I don't think I could truly be myself at a party even if my life depended on it.

This, however, is not something Evelyn needs to know.

"Where exactly are you living?" she asks.

"Studio City. I'm sharing a condo with my best friend from high school."

"Straight down the 101 for work and then back home again. No wonder you've only seen concrete. Didn't anyone tell you that you should have taken an apartment on the Westside?"

"Too pricey to go it alone," I admit, and I can tell that my admission surprises her. When I make the effort—like when I'm Social Nikki—I can't help but look like I come from money. Probably because I do.

Come from it, that is. But that doesn't mean I brought it with me.

"How old are you?"

"Twenty-four."

Evelyn nods sagely, as if my age reveals some secret about me. "You'll be wanting a place of your own soon enough. You call me when you do and we'll find you someplace with a view. Not as good as this one, of course, but we can manage something better than a freeway on-ramp."

"It's not that bad, I promise."

"Of course it's not," she says in a tone that says the exact opposite. "As for views," she continues, gesturing toward the now-dark ocean and the sky that's starting to bloom with stars, "you're welcome to come back anytime and share mine."

"I might take you up on that," I admit. "I'd love to bring a decent camera back here and take a shot or two."

"It's an open invitation. I'll provide the wine and you can provide the entertainment. A young woman loose in the city. Will it be a drama? A rom-com? Not a tragedy, I hope. I love a good cry as much as the next woman, but I like you. You need a happy ending."

I tense, but Evelyn doesn't know she's hit a nerve. That's why I moved to LA, after all. New life. New story. New Nikki.

I ramp up the Social Nikki smile and lift my

champagne flute. "To happy endings. And to this amazing party. I think I've kept you from it long enough."

"Bullshit," she says. "I'm the one monopolizing you, and we both know it."

We slip back inside, the buzz of alcohol-fueled conversation replacing the soft calm of the ocean.

"The truth is, I'm a terrible hostess. I do what I want, talk to whoever I want, and if my guests feel slighted they can damn well deal with it."

I gape. I can almost hear my mother's cries of horror all the way from Dallas.

"Besides," she continues, "this party isn't supposed to be about me. I put together this little shindig to introduce Blaine and his art to the community. He's the one who should be doing the mingling, not me. I may be fucking him, but I'm not going to baby him."

Evelyn has completely destroyed my image of how a hostess for the not-to-be-missed social event of the weekend is supposed to behave, and I think I'm a little in love with her for that.

"I haven't met Blaine yet. That's him, right?" I point to a tall reed of a man. He is bald, but sports a red goatee. I'm pretty sure it's not his natural color. A small crowd hums around him, like bees drawing nectar from a flower. His outfit is certainly as bright as one.

"That's my little center of attention, all right," Evelyn says. "The man of the hour. Talented, isn't he?" Her hand sweeps out to indicate her massive living room. Every wall is covered with paintings. Except for a few benches, whatever furniture was once in the room has been removed and replaced with easels on which more paintings stand.

I suppose technically they are portraits. The models are nudes, but these aren't like anything you would see in a classical art book. There's something edgy about them. Something provocative and raw. I can tell that they are expertly conceived and carried out, and yet they disturb me, as if they reveal more about the person viewing the portrait than about the painter or the model.

As far as I can tell, I'm the only one with that reaction. Certainly the crowd around Blaine is glowing. I can hear the gushing praise from here.

"I picked a winner with that one," Evelyn says. "But let's see. Who do you want to meet? Rip Carrington and Lyle Tarpin? Those two are guaranteed drama, that's for damn sure, and your roommate will be jealous as hell if you chat them up."

"She will?"

Evelyn's brows arch up. "Rip and Lyle? They've been feuding for weeks." She narrows her eyes at me. "The fiasco about the new season of their sitcom? It's all over the Internet? You really don't know them?"

"Sorry," I say, feeling the need to apologize. "My school schedule was pretty intense. And I'm sure you can imagine what working for Carl is like."

Speaking of …

I glance around, but I don't see my boss anywhere.

"That is one serious gap in your education," Evelyn says. "Culture—and yes, pop culture counts—is just as important as—what did you say you studied?"

"I don't think I mentioned it. But I have a double major in electrical engineering and computer science."

"So you've got brains and beauty. See? That's something else we have in common. Gotta say, though, with an education like that, I don't see why you signed up to be Carl's secretary."

I laugh. "I'm not, I swear. Carl was looking for someone with tech experience to work with him on the business side of things, and I was looking for a job where I could learn the business side. Get my feet wet. I think he was a little hesitant to hire me at first—my skills definitely lean toward tech—but I convinced him I'm a fast learner."

She peers at me. "I smell ambition."

I lift a shoulder in a casual shrug. "It's Los Angeles. Isn't that what this town is all about?"

"Ha! Carl's lucky he's got you. It'll be interesting to see how long he keeps you. But let's see … who here would intrigue you …?"

She casts about the room, finally pointing to a fifty-something man holding court in a corner. "That's

Charles Maynard," she says. "I've known Charlie for years. Intimidating as hell until you get to know him. But it's worth it. His clients are either celebrities with name recognition or power brokers with more money than God. Either way, he's got all the best stories."

"He's a lawyer?"

"With Bender, Twain & McGuire. Very prestigious firm."

"I know," I say, happy to show that I'm not entirely ignorant, despite not knowing Rip or Lyle. "One of my closest friends works for the firm. He started here but he's in their New York office now."

"Well, come on, then, Texas. I'll introduce you." We take one step in that direction, but then Evelyn stops me. Maynard has pulled out his phone, and is shouting instructions at someone. I catch a few well-placed curses and eye Evelyn sideways. She looks unconcerned "He's a pussycat at heart. Trust me, I've worked with him before. Back in my agenting days, we put together more celebrity biopic deals for our clients than I can count. And we fought to keep a few tell-alls off the screen, too." She shakes her head, as if reliving those glory days, then pats my arm. "Still, we'll wait 'til he calms down a bit. In the meantime, though ..."

She trails off, and the corners of her mouth turn down in a frown as she scans the room again. "I don't think he's here yet, but—oh! Yes! Now *there's* someone you should meet. And if you want to talk views, the house he's building has one that makes my view look like, well, like yours." She points toward the entrance hall, but all I see are bobbing heads and haute couture. "He hardly ever accepts invitations, but we go way back," she says.

I still can't see who she's talking about, but then the crowd parts and I see the man in profile. Goose bumps rise on my arms, but I'm not cold. In fact, I'm suddenly very, very warm.

He's tall and so handsome that the word is almost an insult. But it's more than that. It's not his looks, it's his *presence*. He commands the room simply by being in it, and I realize that Evelyn and I aren't the only ones looking at him. The entire crowd has noticed his arrival. He must feel the weight of all those eyes, and yet the attention doesn't faze him at all. He smiles at the girl with the champagne, takes a glass, and begins to chat casually with a woman who approaches him, a simpering smile stretched across her face.

"Damn that girl," Evelyn says. "She never did bring me my vodka."

But I barely hear her. "Damien Stark," I say. My voice surprises me. It's little more than breath.

Evelyn's brows rise so high I notice the movement in my peripheral vision. "Well, how about that?" she says knowingly. "Looks like I guessed right."

"You did," I admit. "Mr. Stark is just the man I want to see."

I hope you enjoyed the excerpt! Grab your own copy of Release Me ... or any of the books in the series now!

The Original Trilogy
Release Me
Claim Me
Complete Me
And Beyond...
Anchor Me
Lost With Me

More Nikki & Damien Stark

Need your Nikki & Damien fix?

Not only is *Please Me*, a 1001 Dark Nights Nikki & Damien Stark novella releasing August 28, 2018, but there's a brand new *full length* Nikki & Damien book coming in 2018, too!

Lost With Me
Stark Saga, Book 5
Coming Fall 2018

Some rave reviews for J. Kenner's sizzling romances...

With Kenner's heartfelt and beautiful writing, she captures the true raw emotions of her characters as they battle with their feelings.—Michelle from Four Chicks Flipping Books on *Hold On Tight*

An unexpectedly gritty and raw second chance romance that's hot, sexy and full of surprises—MammieBabbie on *Hold On Tight*

Holy sexual tension, Batman! Being inside the heads of these two lust-struck characters had me turning on the fan in winter!—iScream Books Blog on *Down On Me*

Sexy. Sassy. Fun. *Down On Me* is the perfect start to The Man of the Month series and I'm already jonesing for more!!—Heather from White Hot Reads on *Down On Me*

I just get sucked into these books and can not get enough of this series. They are so well written and as satisfying as each book is they leave you greedy for more. — Goodreads reviewer on *Wicked Torture*

A sizzling, intoxicating, sexy read!!!! J. Kenner had me devouring Wicked Dirty, the second installment of *Stark World Series* in one sitting. I loved everything about this book from the opening pages to the raw and vulnerable characters. With her sophisticated prose, Kenner created a love story that had the perfect blend of lust, passion, sexual tension, raw emotions and love. - Michelle, Four Chicks Flipping Pages

Wicked Dirty CLAIMED and CONSUMED every ounce of me from the very first page. Mind racing. Pulse pounding. Breaths bated. Feels flowing. Eyes wide in anticipation. Heart beating out of my chest. I felt the current of *Wicked Dirty* flow through me. I was DRUNK on this book that was my fine whiskey, so smooth and spectacular, and could not get enough of this *Wicked Dirty* drink.   - Karen Bookalicious Babes Blog

"Sinfully sexy and full of heart. Kenner shines in this second chance, slow burn of a romance. Wicked Grind is the perfect book to kick off your summer."-

K. Bromberg, New York Times bestselling author (on Wicked Grind)

"J. Kenner never disappoints~her books just get better and better." - *Mom's Guilty Pleasure (on Wicked Grind)*

"I don't think J. Kenner could write a bad story if she tried. ... Wicked Grind is a great beginning to what I'm positive will be a very successful series. ... The line forms here." *iScream Books (On Wicked Grind)*

"Scorching, sweet, and soul-searing, *Anchor Me* is the ultimate love story that stands the test of time and tribulation. THE TRUEST LOVE!" *Bookalicious Babes Blog (on Anchor Me)*

"J. Kenner has brought this couple to life and the character connection that I have to these two holds no bounds and that is testament to J. Kenner's writing ability." *The Romance Cover (on Anchor Me)*

"J. Kenner writes an emotional and personal story line. ... The premise will captivate your imagination;

the characters will break your heart; the romance continues to push the envelope." *The Reading Café (on Anchor Me)*

"Kenner may very well have cornered the market on sinfully attractive, dominant antiheroes and the women who swoon for them . . ." *Romantic Times*

"*Wanted* is another J. Kenner masterpiece . . . This was an intriguing look at self-discovery and forbidden love all wrapped into a neat little action-suspense package. There was plenty of sexual tension and eventually action. Evan was hot, hot, hot! Together, they were combustible. But can we expect anything less from J. Kenner?" *Reading Haven*

"*Wanted* by J. Kenner is the whole package! A toe-curling smokin' hot read, full of incredible characters and a brilliant storyline that you won't be able to get enough of. I can't wait for the next book in this series . . . I'm hooked!" *Flirty & Dirty Book Blog*

"J. Kenner's evocative writing thrillingly captures the power of physical attraction, the pull of longing, the universe-altering effect one person can have on another. . . . *Claim Me* has the emotional depth to back up the sex . . . Every scene is infused with both erotic tension, and the tension of wondering what lies beneath Damien's veneer – and how and when it will be revealed." *Heroes and Heartbreakers*

"*Claim Me* by J. Kenner is an erotic, sexy and exciting ride. The story between Damien and Nikki is amazing and written beautifully. The intimate and detailed sex scenes will leave you fanning yourself to cool down. With the writing style of Ms. Kenner you almost feel like you are there in the story riding along the emotional rollercoaster with Damien and Nikki." *Fresh Fiction*

"PERFECT for fans of *Fifty Shades of Grey* and *Bared to You*. *Release Me* is a powerful and erotic romance novel that is sure to make adult romance readers sweat, sigh and swoon." *Reading, Eating & Dreaming Blog*

"I will admit, I am in the 'I loved *Fifty Shades*' camp, but after reading *Release Me*, Mr. Grey only scratches the surface compared to Damien Stark." *Cocktails and Books Blog*

"It is not often when a book is so amazingly well-written that I find it hard to even begin to accurately describe it . . . I recommend this book to everyone who is interested in a passionate love story." *Romance-bookworm's Reviews*

"The story is one that will rank up with the *Fifty Shades* and Cross Fire trilogies." *Incubus Publishing Blog*

"The plot is complex, the characters engaging, and J. Kenner's passionate writing brings it all perfectly together." *Harlequin Junkie*

Deepest Kiss

Entice Me

Hold Me

Please Me

The Steele Books/Stark International:

He was the only man who made her feel alive.

Say My Name

On My Knees

Under My Skin

Take My Dare (includes short story Steal My Heart)

Stark International Novellas:

Meet Jamie & Ryan-so hot it sizzles.

Tame Me

Tempt Me

S.I.N. Trilogy:

It was wrong for them to be together…

…but harder to stay apart.

Dirtiest Secret

Hottest Mess

Sweetest Taboo

Shake It Up

All Night Long

In Too Deep

Light My Fire

Walk The Line

Bar Bites: A Man of the Month Cookbook(by J. Kenner &
Suzanne M. Johnson)

Additional Titles

Wild Thing

One Night (A Stark World short story in the Second
Chances anthology)

Also by Julie Kenner

Also by Julie Kenner

Day of the Demon

The Dark Pleasures Series:
Caress of Darkness
Find Me In Darkness
Find Me In Pleasure
Find Me In Passion
Caress of Pleasure

The Blood Lily Chronicles:
Tainted
Torn
Turned

Rising Storm:
Rising Storm: Tempest Rising
Rising Storm: Quiet Storm

Devil May Care:
Seducing Sin
Tempting Fate

About the Author

J. Kenner (aka Julie Kenner) is the *New York Times*, *USA Today*, *Publishers Weekly*, *Wall Street Journal* and #1 International bestselling author of over eighty novels, novellas and short stories in a variety of genres.

JK has been praised by *Publishers Weekly* as an author with a "flair for dialogue and eccentric characterizations" and by *RT Bookclub* for having "cornered the market on sinfully attractive, dominant antiheroes and the women who swoon for them." A five-time finalist for Romance Writers of America's prestigious RITA award, JK took home the first RITA trophy awarded in the category of erotic romance in 2014 for her novel, *Claim Me* (book 2 of her Stark Trilogy).

In her previous career as an attorney, JK worked as a lawyer in Southern California and Texas. She currently lives in Central Texas, with her husband, two daughters, and two rather spastic cats.

More ways to connect:

www.jkenner.com
Text JKenner to 21000 for JK's text alerts.

 facebook.com/jkennerbooks

twitter.com/juliekenner

CPSIA information can be obtained
at www.ICGtesting.com
Printed in the USA
LVOW10s2046200318
570524LV00017B/372/P